# Kingdom Armenia

## Vol. I: Rise of Tigran The Great

## Part I
## The Road to Parthia

## Harry Gazarian

TITLE: Kingdom Armenia - Vol. 1: Rise of Tigran the Great - Part 1: The Road to Parthia
AUTHOR: Harry Gazarian

COVER AND LAYOUT DESIGN: Tânia Gomes (Mystic Wings)
MAP ILLUSTRATION: Najlakay
COVER AND INTERIOR ILLUSTRATIONS: Mitchell Nolte

ISBN: 9781794136106

VISIT US AT
# kingdomarmenia.com

# The Road to Parthia

## Harry Gazarian

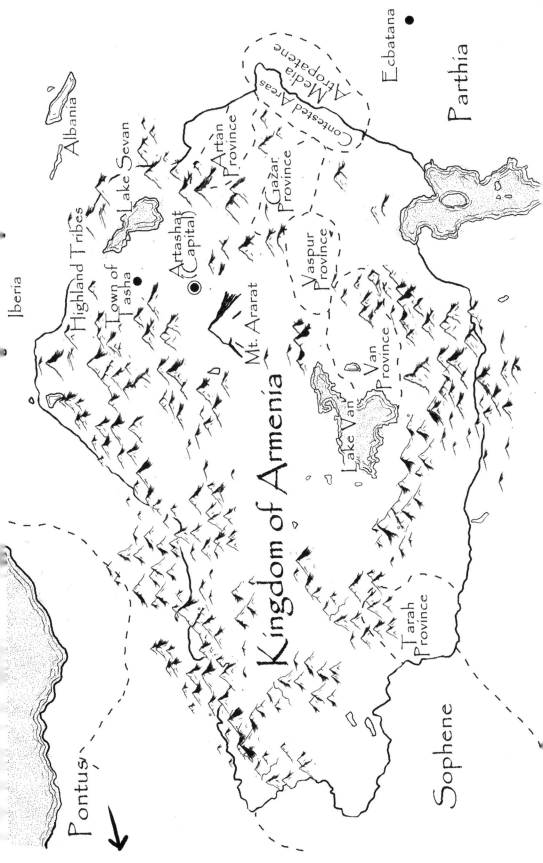

# Chapter One

Young Prince Tigran shifted under his wet cloak. A late afternoon sun tried to break through the clouds up ahead, but he only felt the cold winds pushing at his back.

Tigran ran a hand through his long, damp hair. Beneath him, his horse neighed impatiently. Two weeks of traveling along little-known passages, south through the Great Stormy Mountains, had brought them to the cliff's edge where they now stood. Heavy, wet clouds still hung over the craggy mountain valley their small caravan just crossed. Far in the distance, the Mountains of Ararat stabbed resolutely through a gloomy haze, marking the modest lands of his people.

Scowling, the prince spat the day's grime from his teeth. From here he could survey the entirety of his kingdom with scarcely the need to turn his head in one direction or the other. Armenia, a small kingdom recently brought under the 'protection' of the Parthian Empire, was still a proud land, one that had afforded Tigran a scholar's education and a warrior's training – yet it proffered none of the grandeur, opportunity or might of Parthia. The horse shifted beneath him.

"Easy, there." He patted his horse's neck. "Soon we will both be grazing on greener pastures."

A few pebbles near the beast's hooves tumbled over the edge of the cliff and out of sight. The Prince sighed; the irony was not lost on him. His own kingdom seemed as insignificant as the pebble, precariously perched on the edge of an empire that was entirely capable of nudging them into oblivion. Tigran desired to be part of the mountain rather than an errant rock so easily disposed of.

Parthia – a great, rich empire flowing over the mountains and beyond the horizon -- seemed to stretch to the very edges of eternity. The Prince had visited Parthia six times in almost as many years. At first, the passage itself was adventure enough to sustain him, but now, each time he left there he yearned more desperately to return. On this seventh journey, his yearning was even more unbearable than usual because this time Parthia dangled yet another indulgence to partake of; Roya.

The girl did not belong to a bloodline of any consequence, but in every other way she was anything but common. She was beautiful, but not in the demure way that young royals were supposed to imagine their women. Tigran had been shocked by and then intoxicated with her passion and confidence from the moment he met her. He adored her – and he adored Parthia all the more because she was in it.

Tigran pulled Roya's most recent letter from his tunic. He received it not yet a month ago, but its corners and creases were already softening from the wear of being unrolled and rerolled so many times. Nearly a year had passed since they had seen each other. Her letters always lifted his spirits, but this letter in particular made the Prince ache: she had written that her father would be traveling during Tigran's next scheduled visit to Parthia. Roya would be alone.

Tigran turned his horse south; away from the panorama of his homeland and toward the route they would be taking toward Ecbatana, the summer capital city of the Parthian Empire.

*Oh, my poor, valiant Armenia, what are you next to the most powerful, most beautiful, most enticing Empire on earth?*

His copper eyes glistened. *Only a few more days...*

"Tigran, really, all alone again?" came an amused voice from behind him. "You seem to have misplaced your caravan, your captain, the horses, the carts, the Guard, your servants..."

The Prince was startled from his wistfulness and quickly concealed Roya's letter before turning to greet his friend.

"Bakar, don't think I didn't hear you approaching. I wanted...I was hoping to find a bit of warmth from the sun before it sets. That accursed rain – "

"Has stopped for now, gods be praised," interrupted Bakar with a mischievous grin, "but the damp is about to be the least of your worries. Harat is looking for you, and he is displeased that you have wandered off *again*. I came to warn you of the severe tongue-lashing that is headed your way."

Tigran smiled at his friend. Although there was nearly three years between them, young Bakar was the Prince's closest companion. As an infant, Bakar had been abandoned on the doorstep of the Royal Guard's barracks. Two elderly women, both workers in the barracks' kitchen, had stumbled upon the bassinet one otherwise unremarkable evening and had taken pity on the orphaned child, raising him there among the men of the Royal Guard.

The horses' ears pricked and moments later Tigran heard the sound of tapping hooves echoing over the rocky terrain. He nudged his horse to face three armored riders approaching. As they neared, two of the riders slowed their pace and eventually stopped. The third rider pressed on. Tigran knew who it was well before his features came into view.

Beyond the two riders who kept their distance, the Prince could make out the first of the work animals and their handlers rising over the hilltop through the gap in the bluffs. Even from this distance they looked overburdened, not only by the loads of raw copper and bronze they carted, but also from the hard traveling and unforgiving weather.

The lone rider cantering towards them pulled his mount to a halt.

While the Prince was discreetly clad in his faded tunic and a dark cloak, Captain Harat, Chief of the Royal Guard and Sworn Protector of Armenia, wore gleaming bronze plates over his thick leather armor. An ostentatious red and yellow cape was fastened at his collar and at his hip hung a long sword in an elaborately carved silver sheath. Over his shoulder was a four-foot-long oak bow. Atop his head was a polished bronze helmet that might have hidden the warrior's age, were it not for the thick, salty beard protruding from his jaw.

"Sire, we've entered troubled areas," Harat growled, his voice even more authoritative than usual. "As I told you earlier, we have crossed into ancient Median territory. It would be best to stay with the group. The horses are tired and the last of the sun is about to leave us to fend for ourselves on this damnable mountain."

Any onlooker would believe Captain Harat to be quite the spectacle, but Tigran knew his old mentor called attention to himself only to divert it away from the Prince while they journeyed through dangerous lands.

"My apologies, Captain," replied the Prince. "You are right; it would be best to get moving again."

"Moving!" Harat chortled. "Forgive me Sire, but it is far too dangerous to attempt travel through these hills in the dark! You know as well as I that Media is infested with tribes of bandits and insolent savages that have no love for us. We need to secure the shipment before nightfall – that is, unless you'd prefer to turn up before the King of Kings empty-handed?"

Tigran's heart sank. Stopping now meant further delaying their arrival at Ecbatana.

"Well," he muttered, "we certainly can't make camp here out in the open. Perhaps it would be better to press on awhile yet."

"Sire," Harat said, "we must make our way back to the path – if we can find it – and down this mountain to a more concealed area. Scouts have brought word that the outbreak of banditry in the area has risen steadily. Some of the southernmost villages have already been raided and merchants are altering their routes to avoid their treachery. Hurry now, you two!"

Tigran and Bakar obediently followed Captain Harat back to the trail, but the Prince left several paces between them and their leader. When the Captain was safely out of earshot, the Prince spoke softly over his shoulder to Bakar.

"I do wish we would go on a little further tonight. At this pace I fear we will never get there!"

"I understand," whispered Bakar, his eyebrows raised, "but you know Harat is right, as usual. How would it look if you arrived in Ecbatana wounded? Or worse, with no tribute? Especially *this* time."

The Prince begrudgingly agreed that his companions were correct. Besides themselves, a handful of men of the Royal Guard and some servants, they had with them twenty breathtaking Caspian horses as well as eight donkeys, weighted down with rolls of copper and bronze, an addition to the year's tribute. It would indeed be better to show up on King Mithridates' doorstep intact and bearing gifts rather than not arrive at all or, worse, to arrive without the King's tribute.

The Prince tried not to think too much about the other thing Bakar alluded to; that *this* time, the King of Kings wanted to personally meet with Tigran after they arrived. It was pressure enough to be spending his first night alone with Roya, but added upon that was a meeting with the ruler of the entire Parthian Empire. With the opportunity to face two of his most cherished dreams at once, Tigran knew he should be elated, but in fact, he was uneasy. Suddenly he wasn't in as much of a hurry to get there...

"Make haste, gentlemen!" the Captain barked over his shoulder at Tigran and Bakar, who were now trailing at a considerable distance. "We must move quickly. This night threatens to be starless."

---

Tigran lay alone in his tent. Their descent had been harrowing in the dark and everyone had long since retired to their sleeping quarters. But slumber evaded the Prince. The allure of Parthia, of Mithridates' favor, of the enchanting and unchaperoned Roya was merciless. His thoughts ran possible scenarios for each meeting, contemplating both good and bad outcomes for each.

Tigran shut his eyes and willed his body to relax. *The sooner I fall asleep, the quicker dawn will come and we can resume travel.* But his mind would not let him rest. Nor did he want to reveal the source of his anxiety and impatience to anyone, even Bakar, his closest friend.

Bakar revered their homeland and its royal family for permitting him to be raised, trained, and educated there. The two had met in the barracks during training when they were both young boys under the tutelage of Captain Harat. Tigran recalled admiring the orphan's determination in spite of his small size. They quickly became fast friends.

It wasn't long before most of Harat's students had surpassed Bakar in size and strength, yet none of them – not even Tigran – could match his devotion to his duties and the Crown. Everything Bakar undertook was colored by his allegiance to the land that had saved his life – including, it seemed, his friendship with the Prince.

Tigran sighed. He cared for Armenia too, of course, but Bakar's unflinching loyalty somehow shamed him, and so, he had become more reserved about sharing his growing affection for Parthia.

Tigran opened his eyes and realized he had, at last, been sleeping, but for how long he could not tell. He looked drowsily at the dancing glow projected onto the canvas above him from the plain clay lamp beside his bed. The fact that there was still oil left in the lamp told him he couldn't have slept too long. So why was he awake now?

He heard the sounds of hoofs stirring about outside, from some of the twenty-odd horses nearby from where he lay, but that was not uncommon so he ignored it. After all, the guard outside his tent would call out an alarm if there was anything amiss.

Then the oil lamp flickered and, at that precise instant, a dark figure stole into the tent and stood motionless just inside of the still rippling flaps of the doorway.

Still coming out of his sleepy daze Tigran blinked hard, but the figure remained. He sat up quickly, which suddenly caused the dark shadow to launch itself towards him.

The light from the lamp glistening briefly on the obsidian daggers in his hands. Tigran had enough time to get to one knee, but not to reach for his weapon; he raised his bare hands out in front of him as a last resort.

The attacker leapt from his side of the bed, daggers out, and knocked Tigran backward with a shockingly strong knee thrust to his chest. As the Prince struggled to regain his balance and breath, he noticed the glint of one obsidian dagger just seconds from being driven into his heart. He reached out and grasped his attacker's forearm, giving it a sharp, agonizing twist away from his body.

His assailant winced and dropped that weapon but managed an awkward swing of the dagger in his other hand toward Tigran's throat. The Prince let go and leaned away in time, but stumbled back and fell over his traveling clothes and boots, laid out for tomorrow's journey.

Tigran struggled to regain his footing as he watched his mysterious attacker move tentatively to retrieve the dagger he'd dropped, his shoulder apparently in pain from the Prince's deflection.

Tigran realized this was no common thief, but a dangerously skilled assassin. He knew this man was not after riches, he was out for blood.

*By the gods, where is my sword?*

He realized then his weapon now lay on the other side of the bed, in front of the crate on which the clay lamp sat. Keeping an eye on the black figure, he jumped over the bedclothes to fetch the sword and in that instant his opponent launched one of his weapons.

The dagger dug into Tigran's side inflicting a painful, bloody gash before glancing off his hipbone and falling to the ground, where it shattered into pieces against an errant rock.

The Prince's knees buckled for an instant and he crumpled on the bedding with his attacker close behind. He reached out blindly, and when his hand touched the oil lamp, he grabbed it, still half buckled over in anguish, and thrust it sharply upward into the attacker's face.

The man screamed as the lamp broke on the bones of his face, sending a shower of hot oil and bits of clay around the tent. Tigran didn't know whether his attacker was burned by the hot oil or cut by the shards of clay, for the tent quickly fell into darkness.

Tigran scrambled off of the bed in the direction of his sword, hoping his assailant was as blinded by the dark as he, and more than a little injured by the hot lamp. Not so – a blow landed squarely on Tigran's right temple; the second one made his knees buckle again and his head reel, but Tigran managed to return a forceful swing in the direction of the first two blows. One caught his attacker on the jaw and Tigran sensed him stumbling backward. The pain of the punch reverberated from Tigran's fist and traveled up his arm, and in that instant the Prince realized with disoriented relief that since his opponent had resorted to using his fists, he must have dropped the second dagger when Tigran smashed his face with the lamp.

He heard people shouting outside, and saw bouncing circles of torchlight enlarging around the tent walls.

With a renewed courage, Tigran took a step forward in the blackness toward the form in front of him. He threw a punch to the assailant's midsection and was rewarded with a grunt of pain. He stepped even

closer and launched a battery of blows to his opponent's stomach until he
backed up and tripped over something, falling backward to the ground.
Tigran threw himself onto the body, locking the man's shoulders down
with his knees. He worked his hands up until he found the man's throat
and then began to squeeze.

The mysterious assailant struggled to free himself, but the Prince
tightened his grip, now driven by the animal ecstasy of the kill. He
smelled the rotten breath of the man beneath him, the stinking puffs of air
slowing as Tigran pressed his fingers deeper into the pulse in the man's
neck, slowing the thrashing until it stopped. Then Tigran felt nothing
but his own ragged breathing accompanied by hard thumping deep in
his chest.

Light had filled into the tent now, and he could hear and feel the
commotion of men surrounding him, but Tigran did not move.

He half realized a deep, panicked voice behind him. "Prince Tigran!"

He waited several moments more, still tightly clenching the man's
neck, scarcely believing it could be over. Tigran still could not focus on
the features of his face, but he could see a large piece of the broken clay

lamp lodged deep in the stranger's eye. Blood ran down from the wound and over Tigran's fingers.

He felt a gentle touch on his shoulder, and an equally gentle voice that said, "Tigran, it's done."

He loosened his hands and waited again. Nothing.

It *was* done. Prince Tigran had killed his first man.

———•—••—•—

Bakar passed around cups of ale and then set his own down on the crate beside him. He knelt to address the wound on Tigran's side again. After recounting the attack to them, his friend had hardly said a word. Even now he did not flinch, though Bakar could see the gash was deep.

"It must have deflected off of the bone," Bakar said softly.

The Prince also suffered a swollen eye and hand, but all in all, Bakar knew his friend had escaped the worst of it.

Captain Harat slammed his cup down on the small table in front of him and cursed.

"My men will pay for such negligence. And me, wasting my time on the other side of camp checking on the accursed tributes, instead of watching over your tent myself! To be sure, I will see that justice is served – to all of us."

Tigran, who was staring at the ale in his hands, shifted a tired gaze toward the Captain.

"Harat, he murdered a guard on perimeter watch and the guard outside my tent. We have already paid the price."

The Captain grunted and swallowed his ale, unappeased.

"He was so quiet he did not even disturb the horses," offered Bakar.

"I myself did not hear him until after the attack had begun," Tigran managed to mutter before returning his gaze to his hands. "If I hadn't opened my eyes when I did..."

The three fell silent. Bakar could see that Harat was anxious to unravel what happened and whose heads would roll because of it – even if one of those heads was his own. Tigran, for his part, was visibly shaken. Every word he uttered seemed to take genuine effort. Bakar imagined that practicing to be a warrior was a very different experience from actual mortal combat. He watched the prince closely as he continued to dress his wound.

"The gash is deep," declared Bakar, "but not serious. It is a miracle that your attacker missed his mark. If the dagger had struck you only slightly closer in, you might have bled to death."

Neither Harat nor Tigran looked to be consoled by the news. Harat stood up and began pacing his small, sparse tent. He stopped abruptly and turned to the Prince.

"Sire – "

"Harat," Tigran interrupted, without lifting his gaze, "I owe my skill in combat to you and none other. It does not matter where you were this night; it was you who delivered me."

The Captain stood there, looking at his charge. Then he returned to his seat and began to ruminate aloud.

"I knew this was a dangerous area, we should have stopped earlier in the day..."

Bakar was thoughtful. "Perhaps the Medians who farm near our border are angry with our rebel Mountain tribes again. Have we heard of any raids there of late?"

"I have heard nothing," said the Prince, barely audible.

A flash of anger crossed Bakar's face.

"It would not surprise me. Our Highlanders are violent and uncivilized. Those infidels dare to call themselves Armenian when they do not even pay tribute to your uncle, the King! It might be possible they did something to provoke the Median farmers to retaliate against the Crown. Perhaps they are trying to get our attention?"

"As everyone knows," said the Captain, "I have no love for those mountain tribes either, but your theory is very doubtful. The altercations between the Medians have been going on well before my own father was born. This is not how they operate. Did you see the body? The man was nude, shaven from head to toe, and caked in a black, chalk-like substance that covered his torso, face, and legs. He used obsidian daggers, sharper than any metal blade, but could be just as deadly for the wielder if not trained properly. No, this was a professional assassin, and a premeditated attempt on the Prince's life, orchestrated by someone who knew where we would be, and when."

Finally, the Prince looked up, his sullen expression replaced by one of shock. At that instant Bakar himself realized the true meaning of the Captain's words.

"You're saying..." Bakar paused, unable to believe the words he was about to utter. "You're saying this was planned by one of our own?"

"It could have been," replied the Captain, "or at the very least, someone with intimate knowledge of the Royal House's schedule must be involved. What's more," he continued, "whoever did this would have to have enough wealth to hire so skilled an assassin."

"So, it could have been any of the many dozens of lords that pass through the palace at any given day?" Tigran said.

"Our suspect would also need enough power to persuade even an assassin to undertake a mission this treacherous and surely suicidal," Bakar added, his mind racing.

"So, one of the many higher lords then?" Tigran mocked.

"I just can't imagine that someone in our kingdom would plan something so disloyal, so sinister," Bakar continued. "The Prince is not even heir to the throne; his father is next in line."

Bakar had a thought but paused before he spoke and, instead, looked at Tigran. It was not something the Prince wanted to hear, of that Bakar was sure. As much as the Prince tried to hide his feelings from him, Bakar knew how his friend favored the Parthian Empire. But it was precisely *because* he was his friend that Bakar had to speak his thoughts.

"The King of Kings also knew," Bakar let out softly.

Tigran turned his head to face him and Bakar averted his eyes to Harat, feeling the shame of it even as he did so.

"Yes, he did at that," Harat thankfully cut in, "as did his pet, our very own ambassador Artaban. I do not trust either of those snakes. But the sad truth of it is, there are a very large number of people who could have arranged this."

"Well that doesn't make me feel any better," the Prince tried to muse again with a half-hearted smile. But his eyes still had that far away gaze.

"I apologize for not laughing, sire," the Captain replied, taking another deep sip of his ale, his brows narrowed in thought and concern.

Suddenly life felt much more dangerous to Bakar. Is this what being an adult was going to be like?

"This is all terribly alarming," Bakar heard himself saying aloud, "what shall we do?"

Captain Harat drank the last of his ale and rose to his feet.

"For now, I'm going to take a couple of guards and do another search around the camp. The remaining guards will still be stationed outside the tent. I doubt there's any need to remind anyone to stay alert after what happened here tonight. Stay here until I return."

Harat turned to the Prince before he left. "You would do well to rest, Your Highness."

Tigran seemed barely to notice the Captain's departure. Bakar studied his friend. He had killed a man tonight — and what a long night it had been. Bakar kept expecting the glow of sunrise to illuminate the tent and put an end to this nightmare.

"My friend, you haven't touched your ale," Bakar said gently.

The Prince said nothing. The darkness persisted.

"Tigran," he tried again, "would you like to try and sleep?"

The Prince produced a joyless laugh and looked directly at his friend.

"Bakar, I can't even close my eyes." He paused for a moment, as if he were once again immersed in the struggle. "One of us had to die tonight; even with all the practice, I was unprepared... it could have easily been me..."

"Unprepared?" said Bakar with a small smile. "If you had been unprepared you would have been killed. Captain Harat has trained you well. You are a fighter, Prince Tigran, a warrior. You have triumphed."

"I don't really know how I feel, but I don't feel triumphant." The Prince stirred his ale with a reed straw. "I'm sorry, I don't wish to think about this anymore, at least not tonight."

"Of course," Bakar replied. He was quiet for a moment, trying to think how best to distract the Prince. "Perhaps you should lie down. Even if you don't close your eyes, it may help refresh you. We still have a handful of days between us and Ecbatana, but we will be there soon enough."

"Ecbatana...yes," said the Prince carefully. "Yes, perhaps I will try to rest after all."

Tigran knelt into bedding nearest him.

Bakar extinguished one of the lamps then took a seat opposite the bed and quietly observed his friend. He was clearly still lost in thought, but his expression had softened now. Then, without warning, he thought he saw a smile cross the Prince's face, though he couldn't be sure in the shadows of the dimly lit tent.

"The sooner you fall asleep..." Tigran mumbled, his eyelids drooping.

Bakar sipped his ale and watched the Prince with curiosity. He was about to inquire regarding Tigran's apparent newfound peace, but before he could, the Prince closed his eyes, relaxed into the bedclothes and, to Bakar's surprise, fell fast asleep.

# Chapter Two

Roya sat next to the window in her bedchamber and absentmindedly twisted a tendril of raven locks through her delicate fingers. The sun's glow had only just begun to spill over the horizon and, even though she knew the Prince would not dare to make an appearance before nightfall, she was nearly vibrating with anticipation. She thought of all the letters from the Prince tucked safely under her mattress. Rereading them would be the least agonizing way to pass the long hours before her, but she wouldn't risk retrieving them until after her father departed on his latest three-day journey to facilitate some trade issues in the east.

Her father had traveled often since he secured his new employment in Ecbatana. In addition to more comfortable surroundings and a second servant for the household, Roya enjoyed the liberty that came from an overprotective father being distracted by frequent business trips, and increasing attention from the King. All she would have to do was dismiss the servants a little earlier than usual and she would be free to do as she pleased when the Prince arrived.

Although she was beautiful by any standard, her honey skin and full, ripe lips had not been enough to make her a contender to marry above her stature, at least not until her father had become a trade emissary for the Royal Court. Most of her friends were long since married off, and Roya suspected strongly that her father worried she would be his charge until the day he died. But a Prince loved her. True, he was only a Prince of one of Parthia's smallest vassal kingdoms, but he was a Prince nevertheless.

She heard a soft knock and turned to find their new servant, a timid but pretty girl, tentatively opening the door.

"What on earth are you doing?" Roya screeched. "Did I give you permission to enter my bedchamber?"

The girl, obviously shocked, made haste to shut the door again and spoke apologetically from the hall.

"I – I am sorry Miss Roya," she stammered. "I thought you were... I didn't expect you to be awake at this early hour."

Indeed, she had not been awake to see the sun rise since before they had gotten the second servant who had taken over the morning chores Roya herself had been tasked with. But she was the lady of the house and she knew she must play her part; the servants were not her friends.

"Well, since I am awake and you have already interrupted me, what is it you want?"

"It's your father, Miss. He is leaving shortly and wishes to speak with you before he departs," came the muffled voice behind the door. "I came to help you dress."

Roya paused dramatically, hoping to suggest to her servant that she was pondering whether or not to relieve her of her duties on the spot for such a careless act. At last she said, "You may enter."

The girl shuffled in with her head bowed shamefully, a simple dress in hand. Roya unfastened her white sleeping smock and let it slide down off her slender shoulders and over the generous curves of her breasts and hips. Her servant helped her into the dress, green with brown embroidery that complemented her eyes. Then she began to carefully run a brush through Roya's long, wavy black hair.

The two were quiet until Roya caught a glimpse of her reflection in the obsidian mirror and scowled at the plainness of what she saw.

"This dress – it's fine to bid my father farewell, I suppose, but I shall want one of my finer gowns ready to wear this evening."

She felt her servant stop the brush mid-stroke.

"I have an engagement," Roya explained quickly, "an important engagement."

"Yes, Miss," the girl replied in an obedient – or was it suspicious? – hush.

Roya was alarmed, but she reminded herself that what she did while her father was away was no one's business but her own – and certainly not any of this servant girl's concern.

"I shall wear the gown with the silk embellishments. After my father leaves, you will see to it that it is ready."

"Yes, Miss," she repeated.

Silence befell them and the girl resumed her work, fastening a few curls away from her mistress' face. Then Roya rose to go downstairs to see her father off. She got as far as the door before turning back. When she spoke, Roya maintained a stern tone, but her dark eyes probably revealed a hint of desperation.

"You will not mention the gown to my father."

"No, Miss," came the timid reply.

Roya left and went downstairs. Her father was already wearing his boots and cloak. He looked impatient.

"My darling girl, how can it possibly take you longer to dress with a servant than without one?" he asked, but Roya could tell he was pleased to see her taking pride in her appearance.

"Father, surely you prefer me to look the part of a royal trade emissary's daughter," she replied with an affected sweetness.

"Roya, for the last time, boasting does not become you. How do you plan to catch a husband when you have become as prideful as a man?"

He paused and his stern expression seemed to belie some secret knowledge.

"At the very least, you should choose a better dress."

Roya's eyes widened.

"Father, I – "

"Here," he interrupted, placing a small box in her hands. "A humble gift for you."

A smile crossed Roya's face as she undid the string, but it disappeared once she removed the lid. Inside the box was a finely crafted copper necklace inlaid with shining stones of red and green. She raised her head to meet her father's gaze and offered a thinly veiled word of thanks.

Her father stepped towards her, placed his hands over her small shoulders and gazed squarely into his daughter's eyes.

"When your mother died and left me alone with you, still a little girl,

I hadn't the faintest idea how to raise you to be the kind of young lady that attracted a wealthy husband. It is fortunate that you are as beautiful as she was – and that my new station affords us a better lot in life."

"Father I..." Roya started.

She wanted to tell him, but she knew what he would think, knew what he would say. That he was just using her for her body, that there was no way a Prince could ever marry someone of such low stature.

But she was sure in her heart it wasn't true. No, she would have to wait until she could prove it for sure, when Tigran *did* ask her to be his wife, then her father would have no choice but to be happy for her.

"What is it my dear?" Her father asked after a moment.

"The necklace is lovely," Roya said, "of course I wished it was silver, but then I suppose the copper does warm the hue of my skin."

He smiled a small smile and folded her into his arms.

"What you lack in grace, my dear, you make up for in ambition. Now, I'm off. Behave yourself if you can."

<hr>

They only passed through the outermost wall of the city, but already the streets were so crowded and noisy that the horses stepped with a disoriented, wary caution. Almost as far as the eye could see, Captain Harat and his caravan were surrounded with carts and animals and people going about sad, impoverished lives.

"Has it really only been seven months since our last excursion to Ecbatana? The city looks much bigger," said Bakar.

"Indeed, indeed!" replied Tigran, who seemed barely able to temper his enthusiasm.

Harat frowned. What appeared to be a bustling city to the two boys looked more like a den of dangerous misfits to the Captain. Pushy merchants and pickpockets alike swarmed about their small contingent. Beggars cried out to them with tattered robes and open palms. Harat also noticed a breed of foreign traders he had never seen before, short and gaunt in appearance, with yellowish skin and narrow eyes.

The entire spectacle made him angry and ill at ease. With the crowds

and the noise, it would be difficult to notice the stirrings of any attacks on their caravan. Harat thought about their cargo and about his young charges. He doubted that the vagrants and charlatans about them would have the wherewithal to organize an assault, but he would feel more secure once they were within the innermost walls of the city where the crowds were thinner.

He turned to the boys who were chattering excitedly to each other.

"My young friends," he said, "do you see that starving child there? Or over there, the drunkard leaning against the wall? Or those merchants shouting over who swindled whom?"

Tigran and Bakar ceased their conversation and looked about them uncomfortably. Then, as they passed through the next gate into a more interior area of the city, the scene changed dramatically. The crowds thinned out now, and the buildings here appeared to be better maintained. Small islands of gardens and trees were strategically placed to form pleasant paths across the huge circular courtyard.

"Ah, and now the poverty is all but forgotten, isn't it?" Harat could only glower at the scene before them. "There, a fat man on his way to another fine meal. Two beautiful women strolling together in their finery. A merchant enticing passerby's with fine incense and oils. Somehow they have all managed to forget what's on the other side of that wall."

The Prince and his friend remained silent as they took in their surroundings.

"Cities beget greed," said the Captain. "Don't forget it. And Sire, let's not forget about the attempt on your life not one week ago. Perhaps it would be better for the pair of you to keep your wits about you rather than gawk at all the distractions."

Harat tried to remember how he felt at their ages; at sixteen and nineteen years of age young men thought they already knew all they needed to know. With little real experience in the world, they could still go about their lives, confident they could face any challenge that could befall them. That was, until an actual complication happened.

As their convoy passed through each successive gate, Harat could feel his spirits begin to lighten. The closer they got to the palace, the safer they became. Finally, they arrived at the innermost gate, built many generations before even Alexander the Macedonian, who himself had passed through this city centuries ago while conquering the Old Persian Empire. Harat tried to imagine a time when this one circular rock wall would have been sufficient to protect the entire summer capital of Old Persia. Over the last several centuries, Ecbatana had swollen in size by five times or more, with as many new walls surrounding it, until this last inner wall had become the ultimate status symbol for its denizens, notwithstanding the palace walls themselves.

In the last few generations the city had come under the control of the Parthians, the inheritors of Old Persia. Harat ground his teeth as he pondered on the life he'd spent fighting them. Armenia did not fight them directly of course; trade and diplomatic negotiations had always been formal with the ruling house of the Parthian Empire, but that wouldn't stop the King of Kings from funding and instigating attacks from their proxy, vassal kingdoms that boarded Armenia. Those many years had seen good men lost, but sadly, the worse was that it had slowly drained Armenia's wealth and divided the Kingdom.

The Captain tried to push back the thoughts of yesterday. After all, it was almost ten years now since Tigran's uncle, King Artavazd, had been pressured by the council, and the urging of young Tigran's very own father, the crowned Prince, to declare the kingdom as Parthia's latest 'ally'. Since then the official standing army had been forced to disband by their new 'protectors', but at least the fighting had largely subsided as well.

Their caravan passed through the final gate and Harat caught a glimpse of Tigran as he marveled at the Palace of the King of Kings, now just a few steps away. Any trace of horror or shame Harat had witnessed cross the Prince's face near the outer walls was nowhere to be seen now. The Captain sighed.

He had known these two boys from the time they were infants, put them on their first horse, handed them their first sword; mentored them. Then, four years past, he had recruited them into the Royal Guard. But the Prince was a man now, and Bakar himself on the cusp; Harat had to hope that whatever impressions his teachings had put on their lives so far was enough, for he realized his influence on them henceforth would be minimal at best.

"Oh," said Bakar, "look over there."

Harat followed Bakar's gaze with his own and scowled at what he saw; Ambassador Artaban.

"And just when we thought we could let our guards down," grumbled the Captain. "Come along. I'm sure the Ambassador is anxious to speak with us."

———•—••—•———

Ambassador Artaban patiently watched the small contingent approach. He was a thin, official-looking man with pitted skin and an aquiline nose. Although he was born in the Armenian capital of Artashat, his role as Ambassador to Parthia meant he seldom ever set foot in his homeland. Instead, he kept busy – and handsomely profitable – overseeing the trade deals and tributes from Armenia on behalf of the King of Kings. Today, it was also his duty to welcome Prince Tigran and his entourage back to Parthia.

He squared himself to his visitors, who were now dismounting from their horses, and pursed his lips into a grin.

"Welcome, Prince Tigran. We are delighted you and your servants have made this long journey to Ecbatana."

Artaban could almost feel Harat tense, but the Prince and his little friend looked pleased enough to see him.

"Ambassador, it is most kind being invited back to this fair city so soon after my last visit," replied Tigran. "Ecbatana holds many treasures I am anxious to explore."

"Indeed, Your Highness, but remember, this is not like your other visits," lisped the Ambassador. "King Mithridates himself has invited you here this time, and he is expecting to meet you in two days' time."

The Prince could not resist a wide smile. "As if I could forget," he said. "I am honored the King of Kings requests an audience with me."

Harat shifted impatiently and interjected, "Though we would prefer to have some idea what he wants."

Ambassador Artaban, still grinning tersely, nodded his head

sympathetically.

"Well, it seems the King's new horses all made it here safely; he will be very pleased for that. But certainly, I understand, it must be vexing to be obliged to travel so far without knowing why. The King of Kings is nothing if not mysterious."

"It is not that mystery that vexes me," Harat replied curtly. "It was the attempt on Prince Tigran's life on our way here."

"What, an assassination attempt on the Prince?" Artaban's hand clutched at his heart and his piercing eyes widened. He looked at Tigran, whose expression was serious, then at the Prince's quiet friend who seemed to simply be studying their exchange. Captain Harat's face was as it usually was; aggressive, accusatory, and engaged.

"Yes," replied Harat, "a skillful and deliberate attack. It is a miracle the Prince lives to tell the tale."

"It is hardly a miracle," said Artaban, dismissing the idea with a wave of his hand. "Our young Prince is a formidable opponent, thanks in no small part to you I'm sure, Captain. I rather wonder who would be foolish enough to pit himself against your talented protégé."

Harat crossed his arms and frowned.

"Who indeed," he said.

Artaban decided to ignore the Captain's thinly veiled accusation. Instead, he faced the Prince with a proud nod.

Prince Tigran smiled at the compliment.

"You are kind for saying so, Ambassador," he offered, "but it was an unsettling experience to say the least."

"A harrowing nightmare, I'm sure," Artaban agreed. "I shall relay this troubling news to the King at once. King Mithridates will not stand for such reckless aggression against one of Parthia's protectorates."

"Certainly," said Harat with an undisguised scoff. "Let us see how your king reacts to the news."

The Ambassador did not flinch.

"He is not *my* king, of course. My king, and yours, is the Prince's uncle," Artaban corrected, "although Mithridates *is* the King of Kings – and it would be best that we all remember that."

Artaban twisted his lips into another smile; he so loved poking the

Captain. He had all the patience in the world for the Prince, even if it was accompanied by hostility from Captain Harat. He was used to it, for it wasn't uncommon for his Armenian brothers to greet him with resentment. After all, Artaban had ascended within the ranks of the greater Parthian kingdom higher than most. He wasn't a noble – he never would be – but he was rich, he was powerful, and he had the ear of the King of Kings. It was a feat that most commoners – and even many nobles – could never dream of.

Prince Tigran looked about himself impatiently. It looked to Artaban that despite his near-death experience, Tigran was beyond pleased to be back amidst the pleasures and vices Ecbatana had to offer – not the least of which was his forthcoming reunion with the new trade emissary's wanton daughter. It was clear from the letters he had intercepted that their romance was clandestine, and it was a secret he was willing to keep, at least until a time came that it proved useful to him.

Finally, Captain Harat said, "Well, let's give the guards and servants a well-deserved rest – that is, once the horses are put away and I can put in place a watch rotation schedule for the night."

Artaban ignored the veiled jibe; as if they'd need security within the inner courtyard of the King's Palace, ha!

The Ambassador turned to the Prince.

"Prince Tigran, enjoy your stay while you are here, and if there is anything you need, please let me know. I will come fetch you the morning of your meeting with the King," then he turned quickly past Harat and added, "and please Captain, let me no longer postpone you from your duties."

As he turned to make his leave, it was all Artaban could do to suppress a laugh.

# Chapter Three

Roya had long since sent the servants to their lower rooms for the evening when she saw the glow from Tigran's torch making its way through the dark, emptied street. Her heart skipped a beat; it would be mere moments now until they were together again.

She glanced nervously into the mirror to be sure that everything was as it should be. Roya and her young servant had spent the better part of the day preparing for her "important engagement." Except for two loose braids that were coiled near the crown of her head, Roya's curls cascaded playfully down her back. Her crimson dress was embellished with lace at her cleavage and around her small waist. She fingered the golden embroidery that adorned the bodice; then carefully smoothed the narrow cuffs of yellow silk. It certainly was not the most beautiful dress she ever seen, but it was the prettiest one she owned. Roya hoped it would please her suitor.

Around her slender neck was the gift she received from her father that morning when he left. She debated wearing it; the necklace was only copper after all, and she feared it would undermine his impression of her as a woman worthy of a Prince. At last she had put it on; the red stones matched her dress and the green ones complemented the flecks in her otherwise dark eyes. It was an adornment that highlighted her beauty, if not her wealth, and finally Roya deemed it worth the risk.

She tiptoed downstairs to greet Tigran at the door before he caused a stir by knocking. Then all of a sudden, there he was. Where just yesterday there had been an interminable, unbearable distance between them, now there was virtually none.

"At last, Prince Tigran," Roya smiled. She almost curtsied, but then decided against it. She was luminous.

"Roya," he said with an exhale that he seemed to have been holding in for months.

Her heart pounded so fiercely she worried the Prince might be able to see it through her chest. In their letters, they had shared their most intimate of thoughts, yet now that the Prince was standing at her doorstep not an arm's length away, she suddenly felt very exposed.

After a moment of simply gazing at her, he took her hand in his. Did Roya see a blush in his cheek? With the last flickers of twilight dancing in the sky, it was impossible to tell.

At last he whispered, "You are the most beautiful thing I have ever set my eyes on."

Gathering her breath back first, Roya softly replied, "And I have never seen a man so attractive."

"You are alone?" Tigran asked.

"Yes. And you?"

"Yes, thanks to Bakar. He did not know where I was going, but I swore him to secrecy and made him promise to help me escape for the night," Tigran said softly. "Harat is determined to keep me out of harm's way after the events of our journey to Ecbatana..."

That was all it took; just a few words between them and the unease of reuniting with a far-flung paramour melted away. Roya grasped his hand more tightly and pulled him inside and upstairs to her bedchamber. Once they were safely inside, she poured two goblets of the wine she procured earlier from the kitchen and stashed in her dressing table.

Handing him a cup, she said, "Tell me."

They sat near each other on two small stools and, by candlelight, Tigran recounted the assassination attempt and his narrow victory.

By the time he finished his account of the fight, Roya was truly horrified.

"Who would do such a thing?" she asked, her voice tinged with panic.

"I wish I knew," said the Prince, "for I doubt seriously that one failed attempt on my life will not engender another."

Roya placed her hand on Tigran's thigh and looked into his eyes with genuine concern.

"Tigran," she said, almost pleadingly, "I did not imagine such things could happen to you. Your words, if I am remembering correctly, were 'I am only a lowly prince of little consequence.' Well, I dare say this is not the way I wanted you to realize those words are not true. Tigran, my Prince, I could not bear to lose you."

The Prince gave Roya a heartfelt look that made her quiver. This was the night they had both been waiting for, their first night – and an unknown enemy almost prevented it from ever happening. He placed one hand over hers and reached out the other to caress her cheek. Roya nestled her lips into his palm and kissed it shyly. She heard the Prince inhale sharply before he gently cupped her chin and drew her mouth onto his.

The kiss set her on fire. It was a kiss fueled by months of waiting, of letters filled with tender promises and words of love. Roya stood up, breathless, and pulled Tigran into her arms. This was her Prince. This was the man who loved her, who had captured her heart, who could one day make her a queen.

Locked in each other's embrace, the Prince's hands moved feverishly over her nubile curves. Roya pressed against him and began reaching up inside his tunic.

"Wait, Roya," murmured the Prince between kisses. "This... I don't know... Is it wise?"

Roya took a demure step backward and gazed up into Tigran's eyes under lowered eyelashes. They each took a breath and she smiled a small, coy smile. She desired this more than anything else she could ever dream, and she wasn't going to let her prince cower away now.

"Tigran, I love you," she said simply.

"And I love you, but what happens after tonight? It will be after winter when I will be able to see you again."

"My love, we have been longing for months for this reunion. You know I am yours forever."

She paused and took a deep breath. Her bosom heaved sensually from beneath her crimson dress, pressing again now against his strong chest.

"But, more importantly, I am yours for tonight."

Tigran's breath quickened. He spun her around by the waist and began kissing her neck through her silken mane. His hands reached up and easily unfastened the attire she had chosen for just such a purpose. Her dress dropped down her body until all she had on was the copper necklace from her father, glimmering faintly in the candlelight.

The night that followed was one she would remember for the rest of her life...

# Chapter Four

The morning of Prince Tigran's audience with Mithridates, Harat paced the arcade, hoping he would have an opportunity to speak with Tigran in private before Ambassador Artaban arrived to escort him into the palace. Tigran was simply too eager, and too inexperienced to deal with a King of an Empire. There was no telling what an old viper like Mithridates could do with such overconfidence and naiveté.

"Captain, you've come to wish me luck?" came Tigran's voice from the other end of the arcade.

Harat was relieved to see him, but he wished the Prince didn't sound so elated. Tigran walked toward the Captain and spoke in a lowered voice.

"I must confess, I am somewhat nervous."

"Sire, you must quell your nerves and keep your wits about you," urged Harat. "We do not know what Mithridates wants, but whatever it is, you can be sure his plans are for his benefit and not your own."

Tigran looked taken aback.

"Captain, surely it's possible that the King of Kings may seek what is beneficial for all? I would prefer to hear him with an open mind."

Harat lowered his voice and leaned in toward the Prince. One simply could not be sure who might be listening.

"Prince Tigran, listen to me. Mithridates would not be meeting with you if he didn't believe he could use you for something. He may threaten you, or worse, he may ply you with flattery to get what he seeks. I am old, I have witnessed such scenarios more than once in my lifetime, and I want you to trust that I know of what I speak. He wants Armenia completely tamed under his heal, and he is likely trying to gain your favor to help make it so."

Tigran shook his head.

"I'm not sure it will all be as sinister as you anticipate, Captain, and I do wish *you* could trust that I am not so wholly inexperienced and unwise as you seem to believe."

Harat sighed. Triggering the Prince's defenses was not the solution here. He placed a large, battle-scarred hand on Tigran's shoulder.

"Indeed, Sire, you are wise beyond your years – but eagerness can undermine even the most profoundly wise of men. Mithridates will not be seeking a dialog, a middle ground. He is only trying to find out in what way you can best serve his interests. And I have witnessed what happens to those he uses when they are no longer useful to him."

The Prince took a nervous breath and nodded his head, seemingly in understanding, but before he could reply, Ambassador Artaban made his appearance.

"Greetings, Sire!" the hawkish little man shouted convivially as he approached. "It is time. Are you ready?"

"I am," said the Prince, straightening up.

"This way, please," gestured the Ambassador with a small nod in Harat's direction.

The two began to make their way toward a set of heavily guarded doors atop a long, heavily decorated stone staircase. Harat was unimpressed that Artaban had all but ignored him and, as he watched the Prince and the Ambassador disappear from view, he tried in vain to fight his growing disquiet about this meeting.

*Thank the Gods for King Artavazd.*

The Prince's uncle and ruler of Armenia, Artavazd was patently unlike the Prince's father, the Crowned Prince, whom Harat believed to be little more than a Parthian pawn, like their own Ambassador. King Artavazd was fiercely loyal to Armenia and had done his utmost to instill that loyalty in his nephew, even now as he approached his final season of life.

Harat could see plainly how the Prince was tempted by the pomp for which the King of Kings was famous, and by the experiences a seemingly endless Empire could afford. For his own part, he did what he could to foster Tigran's loyalty to his homeland, but Harat was not part of the royal bloodline, and the older his young charge became, the more he seemed to be slipping away from him.

Harat spat bitterly. He could do nothing now but hope that the influence of Tigran's ailing uncle, coupled with his own, would be enough to win out over his weak-willed father, that snake of an ambassador, and the cunning King of Kings of Parthia. The future of Armenia might depend on it.

———•—••—•———

Tigran followed behind the Ambassador, the sound of boots on granite floors echoing in his ears. The candle-lit corridor through which they traveled was lined with exquisite tapestries and elaborately carved columns, coated in silver and gold. Shadows danced up the walls then disappeared into darkness so high up that Tigran couldn't tell where the wall met the ceiling. They were only in a hallway and yet the scene still commanded a reverent, wide-eyed hush.

A commotion at the end of the corridor disrupted the silence. Tigran and Artaban stopped in their tracks as the great doors before them swung open.

Two Immortal Guards ushered through a small, flailing young Parthian bound in chains. Although he was well dressed, his tunic was smeared with sweat and dirt, and as they passed, Tigran saw that his back was covered in torn vertical lines smeared with blood. The young man was shouting so feverishly that Tigran could not make out a word.

The Prince cast a sidelong glance at Artaban, who wore the same pleasant demeanor as when he had greeted him. The Ambassador calmly watched the young Parthian's vain protestations as the Immortal Guards led him back down the corridor and out of sight. Tigran did his best to appear as collected as Artaban, who behaved as though a screaming citizen in irons was something he saw every day. He hoped the Ambassador could not sense his alarm.

Artaban gestured toward the open doors before them.

"His Majesty awaits, Prince Tigran. I wish you a pleasant and fruitful meeting."

"Thank you, Ambassador," replied the Prince.

He hesitated only a moment before turning and walking through the doors and into an expansive room filled with additional Immortal Guards as well as numerous attendants and scribes milling about. Several eunuchs busied themselves on the opposite side of the room, all working in a hurry to do their King's bidding.

The doors behind Tigran shut with a foreboding thud. Scarcely a moment more passed before King Mithridates himself entered the room through the gilded door opposite where the Prince stood.

"Prince Tigran," his deep voice echoed from across the vast room, "a warm welcome. Come and take a seat with me."

Wordless, Tigran obeyed. As he made his way toward the King, he couldn't help but be mildly surprised; Mithridates was shorter than he had imagined, but his presence seemed a hundred times larger. His air of confidence effortlessly commanded the attention – even fear – of all within sight.

"I offer my humble greetings, Great King of Parthia," Tigran stammered out as he approached, "and a most ardent word of thanks for the honor of an audience with the King of Kings."

This part of the room was furnished with two extravagantly carved chairs set atop a plush bearskin rug. Nearby was a crackling fireplace that lit the room cheerfully. The King of Kings turned and offered Tigran a warm smile that was, if not entirely calming, at least somewhat reassuring. Mithridates looked pleased to see him.

"Please, sit," he said, gesturing toward one of the chairs.

Prince Tigran moved toward the chair and waited until the King of Kings seated himself in the opposite chair before taking his own seat. The King then waved an arm and the servants and guards scattered like sparrows frightened by a roll of thunder.

Alone, they sat without speaking as the King looked him over. It couldn't have been more than a few moments, but Tigran fidgeted uncomfortably in the silence.

Mithridates waited; the picture of strength and assuredness in his ornate robes. His oiled hair, the color of smoke, was hidden in part beneath a lavish high-domed crown adorned with a bejeweled star. His camel-colored skin was meaty and robust, and one could imagine the royal lifeblood coursing through his veins. He exuded a wise and fearsome air that demanded respect without the tedium of words. Mithridates was every ounce and unmistakably a King.

"I do hope," the Prince offered, "that you were pleased with our humble addition to the year's tribute."

"Certainly, Prince Tigran. Armenia may be small, but it has much to offer."

The King's demeanor was friendly and light.

"Your homeland is blessed with rich supplies of ore and, of course, your sure-footed mountain horses are always put to good use – which reminds me, we shall require Armenia to increase its gift of horses for the Empire again next summer."

The Prince felt deflated; surely the King of Kings hadn't summoned him to Ecbatana only to ask for more horses?

"As you wish, Your Highness," he replied. "I confess I am anxious to prove my, uh, Armenia's ongoing usefulness to the Parthian Empire, humble as it may be."

"You are an ambitious young man, then, like your father?" the King asked.

"A flattering observation, Sire." Prince Tigran paused to collect his thoughts, fearful that being the nephew to the Armenian King would sentence him to a continued life of little more than a tribute runner for the Empire.

"Though I confess I don't always side with my father in all matters. And of course, as you know, I am not in line to inherit the Armenian throne; that will be my father. However, I want to make plain that I am keen to prove myself a worthy friend to the mighty King of Kings."

"You will have your chance, I am sure," Mithridates replied with a gravelly chuckle. "After all, when your father ascends to the throne, *you* will then be the Crowned Prince, and in time, the next King."

Then the King looked Tigran in the eyes.

"Tell me, what is the general sentiment now toward young Prince Tigran within his own borders?"

The Prince was puzzled.

"Forgive me sire, I'm not entirely sure what you mean, I'm afraid."

"Well, do your people respect you? Do they feel they know you? Do you know them?" asked the King. "You must lay the groundwork for your people to accept you as a leader, readying yourself now for your future succession to the Armenian throne."

The Prince's heart began to race; perhaps the King of Kings had more in store for him after all.

"That will likely be many years still, Your Highness... but to answer your question, I suppose I am well enough liked in Armenia. Although, as you know, our humble nation is currently not entirely united under the Armenian flag."

"Ah, yes," the King reflected, his eyes turning away, "that is yet another burden for a King to deal with."

Then he looked back at Tigran and added more sternly, "But unity is an essential ingredient for strong leadership. You must leverage the assets you have to make unity possible. I myself did not unite my country and grow this empire by failing to take advantage of every opportunity. Parthia's economy and influence grow by the day because the King of Kings is wise enough to listen, learn, and act accordingly."

Suddenly, the image of the young Parthian prisoner, wild-eyed like a trapped animal, sprung to the Prince's mind. He summoned his courage and began slowly.

"Forgive me, Sire, but a pressing question troubles me."

"Please," the King smiled. "Unburden yourself."

"The young man I saw being led from the hall in chains...?"

Mithridates waved a hand of dismissal.

"A rotten fruit on an otherwise fruitful tree. As I'm sure you are aware, being in a position of power means you occasionally attract some untoward attention."

Tigran nodded and now thought on the attempt on his life. He wondered if Artaban mentioned the incident to the King, as he promised.

The King continued, "The boy was a spy sent by a member of my own family, a deceit that wounds me deeply. Greed and lust for power can do wicked things to a man; that boy betrayed my confidence with the same mouth he used to kiss my hand."

"I am appalled," said Tigran. "Your own family..."

The King nodded. "Sadly, our allies – even our family members – tend to forget what we have done for them if we neglect to remind them every so often."

"My uncle, the King, has often counseled me that a leader must always be diligent, lest his labors disappear like an untended garden," mused the Prince.

"Your uncle is a wise man who has taught you well," observed Mithridates.

His large, round eyes were serious and unblinking.

"Indeed," replied the Prince, and leaned forward in his chair. He felt a tinge of guilt about what he was about to say, but there was nobody he could ever say such a thing to, except his father, although Tigran never wanted to give him the satisfaction.

"I only wish he perceived the potential of being part of the Parthian Empire, as I do... His resistance to change is at times infuriating."

The King's lips parted in a wistful smile.

"Though I never met him in person, I have in a way, known your uncle since before you were born, I suppose. Yes, he is a stubborn man, and we have had our...disagreements throughout these many years. But then, loyalty to one's homeland is also an admirable quality, is it not?"

"Doubtless," conceded the Prince quickly, "but is it necessary for loyalty to the Armenian crown to preclude loyalty to the Empire?"

King Mithridates' eyes widened, and he stroked his beard.

"What say you, Prince Tigran?"

"I certainly hope not," Tigran honestly replied...and he watched the King of Kings' mouth curled into a broad smile.

Tigran remembered Harat asking how the King would react to the news of the attempt on his life.

"Great King, have you heard of the attempt on my life during our excursion to Ectabana?" Tigran asked.

"Oh yes, my boy," the King said loudly, "Ambassador Artaban did mention it to me. I hear you easily bested the fiend."

"I sustained some minor wounds," Tigran put in, "but I was the survivor when it was done."

"It is an outrage," the King said, with what seemed to be genuine anger, "I will have word put out that you are a personal favorite Prince of the King of Kings. I have also ordered my guards along the Royal Road to double their patrol ranges."

Then the King's expression changed to that of concern, and he added, "But I heard that your Captain Harat decided not to follow the Royal Road? Does he always take such chances with his Prince?"

"My King," Tigran patiently explained, "Captain Harat is the most honorable and loyal person I know. The fact is, on most of our trips here, unless it is strictly a trade envoy, our people have always taken the shorter route. It saves us about three full weeks of travel time on the whole journey."

"Passing by the Stormy Mountains and the vicious tribes that lurk in its shadows," the King replied, "even I have not bothered intruding into their land, and it's not just because they have extremely little to offer anyone."

Tigran was trying to catalog every instant of this meeting, to remember every word and expression for later examination. But even as he tried, with his continued excitement and nervousness, he realized he could not possibly keep up with the King in conversation and at the same time scrutinize his intentions.

"You are correct of course, my King, the route can be dangerous, but in truth, we have had very little encounters in my lifetime," Tigran said.

"It is good to know you can protect yourself if need be; your Captain has trained you well," the King said. Then he leaned closer and more quietly he added, "but did you ever think the attacker could have been someone on your side? It occurs to me that more people in your own Kingdom would know about those routes you take."

Tigran was impressed by the King's quick thinking.

"You are very wise, my King, you seem to be correct again," Tigran replied, "it is the same conclusion we came to after the incident."

"I hope your faith in your Captain is true, for you will need allies to rid yourself of this problem if need be," the King said, standing now.

Tigran quickly stood as well, nodding in reply.

"It was fascinating to meet you Prince Tigran," the King said, extending his hand, palm down, "I hope you will be back here next summer. I have great hopes for our continued friendship."

"Of course, my King, I am honored that you would have it so," Tigran said quickly.

He then quickly realized the King was waiting for Tigran to kiss his hand. In that instant he hesitated, his mind swirling; he did not want to do this, for it was not in his own customs. But he assumed the King of Kings would be offended if he did not, and so, he convinced himself that he was only doing this to honor the Parthian customs so as not to displease the King of Kings himself.

Tigran brought his lips to the King's meaty hand.

"Thank you again for the honor of our meeting, my King." Tigran said.

Tigran hadn't noticed the King call out or make any gesture, but suddenly an Immortal Guard was with them, holding out an arm, pointing the way towards the great doors of the King's Hall.

# Chapter Five

Captain Harat had gotten up early to get the horses ready. He was impatient to make their leave and get back home. Sadly, it seemed the boys, as well as some of the Guardsmen, were not as eager as he. The sun could already be seen starting to rise above the outer walls, but his group was just now plodding out of their rooms. The Captain did not miss the two meagerly clad women trying in vain to sneak out of a couple of the rooms either. But he decided to look the other way, as he had done the previous night, when he spied the Prince making his way back into his room in the early hours of the morning.

*He is a man now and he is my Prince; it is not my place to baby him any longer.*

But Harat couldn't help but worry him, as he would until his last day.

"Captain Harat," said Bakar, who at least seemed to have slept well, "I believe we are going to be a little late in our departure this morning. Uh, it seems the hot evening offered a restless night for most."

The Captain held in his smile, covering it on the outside with his usual scowl. Bakar had grown into a very bright young man, but lying was not a skill he had yet mastered. Harat wondered what Bakar would say if he confronted him about the Prince sneaking out all night. But he decided to spare the boy.

"Yes, I can see that! I'm going to take a short walk. I expect everyone to be ready to move by the time I get back."

"I will see to it Captain," Bakar shouted back, quickly turning back towards his and the Prince's room.

Harat walked away along the outside walls of the Palace and then turned a corner that went past the grand staircase leading up to the Royal Palace itself. As he rounded the corner, deep in thought, he nearly bumped into another walking past him.

"Apologies," Harat said, as he looked up and saw who it was. By the symbols and metals that adorned his expensive, red-hued leather vest, it was clear this was a highly decorated general in the king's army.

"Yes," the man said. He was tall, lean but muscular with a long, straight-haired mustache and beard. His gaze was fierce. "Are you with the Armenian contingent?"

The Captain was taken aback by the question, but he did not let it show.

"I am Captain Harat; I lead the contingent you speak of."

Now it was the General who seemed taken aback; his eyes widened and his lips twisted into a sneer, but as suddenly as the expression came, it was replaced by what looked more like pity.

"Why, the notorious Captain Harat," the General said, "it was *you* I was coming to find. When the king mentioned the Prince of Armenia was here, I wondered if you would be at his side."

"I'm sorry," Harat said, "do I know you?"

"I am General Sanbel, recently appointed as Protector of the Empire's Western Quarter. And I do not believe we have ever met face-to-face, but I am sure we shared the same battlefield a few times in years past. After all, it was you who killed my cavalry leader in battle. Maybe you remember him? He was Captain Vologas, my mentor and leader when I was still a young man."

Harat could not remember ever hearing either of their names – an unfortunate outcome for anyone who'd fought in as many battles as he had – but it was clear this General Sanbel knew about him.

"Apologies, I fought many men in my long life," Harat said, "many good, honorable men. But I could not hope to know most of their names."

"It was at the battle of Green Hill Pass," the General pressed on. "You lead a handful of your heavily armed horsemen in wedge formation, smashed your way around the edge of our right flank, and charged straight at the center. In the confusion that followed, the flank collapsed and your footmen quickly plunged forward. The rout was quick and concise. But during the retreat, Captain Vologas saw you approaching. Instead of turning to flea with the rest of his army, he stood to face you."

Harat remembered it now, it was one of those many battles he thought he would never get out of alive.

The General took a breath, but it seemed he was not finished.

"You dismounted your horse and dropped half your armor to the ground as you marched toward my mentor, sword in hand. When you noticed he was not going to flee, you called out for your men to not interfere. I heard him say, as he was standing there waiting for you to reach him, 'I, Captain Vologas, will not be taken alive! I challenge you, the great General Harat, leader to leader!' Then, as shaming as it is for me to say, as I myself was fleeing, the last thing I heard *you* yell out was, 'Give this man a sword!'"

General Sanbel finally finished his story. He was breathing heavily now, but the puffing of his chest did nothing to intimidate Harat. As far as he was concerned, this man was angry at himself for his cowardly act of self-preservation, the dishonorable act of not staying back with his leader and mentor. Harat wondered how such a man could ever reach such an important position in the Empire.

What Sanbel had *not* heard was Harat trying to calmly talk Vologas down as he was walking up to him and before the challenge was made; and what Sanbel had *not* stayed to witness was the spectacular duel that followed. Harat sustained a few lasting injuries from that fight, and in the end, had considered himself lucky when he was able to force his opponent's weapon from his grip. Harat again had no intention of killing Vologas, but when he realized it was over, the resolute warrior had pulled out a small dagger and sliced his own neck open from ear to ear before he could stop him. Harat had made sure that the Captain's body was returned home with the full honors warranted of a valiant warrior.

"Captain Vologas was an honorable man, but he lost the battle and did not wish to surrender or be captured, and I would not deny him his challenge when he demanded it," Harat replied, his expression painfully neutral. "But in the end, he took his own life."

The General sucked in a deep breath, his right hand made an ever so slight twitch closer to the sheathed sword at his left hip. Harat did not flinch.

After an awkward moment of silence, the General finally made his decision.

"So," General Sanbel said with a counterfeit smile, "you *do* remember him; I thought an old soldier as you, with so many battles and kills, could not hope to remember them all."

"It is an unfortunate thing, every man who falls in battle deserves to be remembered," Harat said with no malice.

"He is remembered, through me," the General replied. "But he would have made a greater general and served the Empire well, if he had lived."

Harat waited a breath, and then said, "I'm sure the Captain would be proud that his protégé has at least been able to achieve that feat."

"Yes," the General said through gritted teeth, "in the years since, my blade has tasted the blood of many men, some better than even you or Vologas ever were. I maneuvered my way up through the ranks, and through whoever stood in my way. I received many promotions, won numerous battles, and have grown a formidable army that is beholden to me...But most importantly, I will never run again."

Again, Harat waited a moment more before he said, "Well, that is good, for a General not to run I mean. Now, I apologize, but it is time we make our leave. It was good meeting you General."

"Ah yes," the General pressed him again, "I forgot that you are no longer a general yourself. It is truly a pity that the great Harat, protector of Armenia for all those years, has now been reduced to caravan guard duty. It must be difficult getting old."

Harat looked the General in the eye.

"Well, perhaps if you are wise, you may be able to experience it for yourself one day," he said.

"Yes, but perhaps I am not yet *that* wise," the General said.

The General quickly moved his hand to the hilt of his sword, but he did not draw the blade. Captain Harat's hand was already on the hilt of his own, but he also did not draw his weapon.

A few long, silent moments passed as they stared each other down.

"Captain Harat! Captain Harat, we're ready!" young Bakar shouted from around the corner.

"Yes," the General once again began, "I will no longer keep you from your work, *Captain* Harat. I must admit, meeting you in person was not as compelling as I had thought it would be."

"General," Harat replied, "if we ever have the pleasure to meet again, I promise to try and make it as captivating as possible."

"Yes," the General said with a nod and a sneer. Before he turned to leave, he added, "perhaps you may have that chance one day."

———•••—

Roya looked furtively over her shoulder through the commotion of the market square. In every direction were vendors shouting over their colorful wares, clamoring for buyers to peruse their collections of glittering jewelry, clay pots and utensils, fragrant fruits, heaps of grains, exotic fabrics and tapestries. On any other day, Roya would be delighted to spend the afternoon shopping with the allowance her father always gave her before his departures. Today, however, she had her heart set on a loftier prize.

Her feeble old servant ambled several paces ahead, her arms already heavily laden with baskets heaped with fresh vegetables and flour for the evening meal. Roya had made up an excuse to accompany her on the shopping trip; the old abandoned temple grounds where she was to meet Prince Tigran lay just on the outskirts of the market.

She caught up with the old woman, who was sweating from the exertion of walking through the harsh afternoon sun burdened with her purchases.

"Go find the butcher," said Roya. "I'd like to surprise father with a meal of chicken upon his return. I have other matters to attend to; I shall meet you back at home."

"Yes, Miss." The old woman managed a tired nod before turning with her heavy packages and making her way through the crowd like a beast of burden ready to be put out.

When Roya was certain her servant was out of sight, she swept through the crowd and into the shadows of the crumbling temple ruins. The Prince was already there.

"Tigran, I have been counting the hours," she said, her voice coquettish. She stepped into his arms and kissed him deeply. This was the last time they would see each other again for many months; she knew she had to make it count.

"As have I," said the Prince when she withdrew her lips.

Roya caressed his neck and played with the laces of his tunic. "I cannot bear the thought of your departure. These months apart are bitter agony."

"I know," said Tigran, cupping her cheeks in his hands, "but I do have one small bit of news that I hope will cheer you. I daresay my audience with Mithridates went about as well as possible. I do believe that your beloved may be able to secure a place in the court of the King of Kings when I return at winter's end."

Roya squealed with glee and wrapped her slender arms around Tigran's neck, her fingers running playfully through his hair.

"Oh, Tigran, that is the most wonderful news! Imagine, the two of us living in the city! I could see you every day..."

"Yes, it almost seems too good to be true," whispered the Prince as he held her, his lips brushing softly against her ear. Roya's breath quickened as she imagined this very moment happening every day of her life – and not just as the daughter of a trade emissary, but as the wife of a prince... yes, a princess, perhaps even one day a queen.

Roya shivered in the ecstasy of Tigran's touch and imagined the day where her finest copper baubles could be discarded with the household rubbish as they were replaced with more gold jewelry than she could ever want. All she had to do was fill these final moments together with memories sweet enough to last the next few months.

Tigran's hands slid down over her hips, then up to rest on the small of her back. He leaned in to kiss her again, but Roya pulled away from him with an inviting smile and tugged gently on his elbow. She led him in the direction of what was left of a large temple column, wide enough to shield them from view of any passersby who chanced to be coming or going from the market.

Once they were safe from the outside world, she would press into him again until he was intoxicated by her warmth, her scent. She would be with him just until it would be impossible for Tigran to forget what it was like to hold her, to taste her, to be one with her again. When it was time to say goodbye, she would make sure to be the one to leave first, so he would have to watch her walk away, wanting.

# Chapter Six

———————

(South-Eastern Armenia, Vaspur Province)

Artos was returning from his tax collecting duties when he saw a fancy carriage and a group of Royal Guards mulling about outside of his family home. Evidently the Crowned Prince, the elder Tigran, was visiting his father again.

His father, Lord Martz, was head of the House of Vaspur, and thus ruled over one of Armenia's Provinces that profited most by trade with Parthia. And of course, that made the Crowned Prince, an outspoken Parthian sympathizer, his father's natural ally.

Artos pulled his horse to a stop, and behind him, his small contingent of strong-arms did the same.

"Devo, secure the coin in the armory and disperse the men," Artos said to his trusted first, "I will go on alone from here."

"Yes, my Lord," Devo replied, turning his mount and relaying the order to the men.

They did as they were told and Artos slipped off the road and made a wide circle to the back of the house. After securing his horse, he soft stepped up to the wall - his head reaching just under the dining wall windows - and listened intently.

"...Trust me," Artos heard the voice of the Crowned Prince saying, "my brother will not likely survive the winter, he is living his last days. Soon we will be able to change the rest of his stifling policies against Parthia, and your coffers will be spilling over."

"You will be King," this was Artos' father speaking now, "what am I to do if you suddenly forget your promises to me then. And I am still flanked by these irritating Provinces that are loyal to the old King's policies."

"You have been by my side for these many years now, Lord Martz," Crowned Prince Tigran replied, "I have promised to make you Chief Royal Adviser to the King, and I will keep that promise. I will still have need of your valuable council."

"And my wealth, if there is any left by then" his father said, "And my eldest son?"

"As I also pledged, your eldest son will be chosen as the next Captain of my *new* Royal Guard. And do not fret about those Provinces around you, they may be bitter and displeased, but they will have to conform; after all, it will be the will of their King."

"Does not your son, Prince Tigran, have his eye on Captaining the Royal guard after Harat?" Artos' father asked next.

"My son will be the new crown prince when I am king; that position will be beneath him. But know that after only my son, will you and yours be my next closest allies."

Artos tried to hold in his anger. He was already aware of everything he just heard, but being reminded that his father and older brother were going to be living in the Capital and have the ear of the King while he would be stuck here collecting copper coins from haggard farmers, really spurred his rage. Sure, he would be the acting Head of the house while they were away, and get to rule over their Province, but he would not be a *real* ruler. That was certainly not good enough for Artos' lofty goals.

"I am with you still, my Prince" his father said then, "we will continue to patiently await the better days you have promised us for so long now."

"They will come, my friend, they will come," the Crowned Prince replied, "I must make my leave now, back North to the Capital. My son should be returning soon from Ectabana and I endeavor to find out about his meeting with the King of Kings."

Artos grunted out his anger this time, then, worried that he may have been heard, stealthily made his way back around the corner and doubled back to his horse.

As he walked his horse to the corral, Artos' thoughts went back to that fateful week, three years past now, when he had gone to the Capital. It was a time he would never forget, especially that last day...the day he made the decision that would shape the rest of his life.

When Artos had first arrived at the capital city of Artashat, it seemed even more glorious than he ever dreamed. The city walls stood above two converging rivers that surrounded it on three sides. On the isthmus, a main road crossed a wide trench before it ended at the largest of the many gates along the palisade. The King's palace could be seen from all angles before even nearing the city, sprawling along the highest hill.

His family had been invited, by the Crowned Prince himself, to attend some Royal function in the King's Palace. It was the first time, and only time since, that his father brought the whole family with him to the capital, and a younger Artos, along with his mother and younger brother, were very excited about the trip.

While there, they were also going to be picking up his older brother, who had just finished training in the Royal Guard for the past year. But more importantly, Artos was himself to be considered for acceptance into the Guards' training program. He was to spend the week with other possible initiates at the Guard barrack grounds just outside the city walls.

Artos remembered again now how that evaluation week had begun; with Prince Tigran, the Crowned Prince's son by the same name, greeting him at the gates with his smug smile, telling him how well his brother had performed, then leading him to that old, worn warrior, Captain Harat. The Prince looked to be a year or two younger than Artos, and the Captain was probably a hundred years older. Artos still recalled how neither of them had impressed him much.

"Lord Artos!"

Devo's calling out from the back road returned Artos to the present. "How goes it?" Artos replied.

"Everything is secure, my lord," Devos said. "And the men have retired for the day. Will there be anything else, sire?"

"No, my friend, that will be all, now go and rest for the night," Artos called out with a last wave.

Later, when he was walking back to the main house, Artos saw the Crowned Princes' carriage and his guards trailing away. He was fully aware that was the next king leaving his family home. He was also aware that the Prince was not just mere friends with his father, but rather, he needed his wealth, and he needed to keep his allies in the south strong. The Crowned Prince made promises to his father and older brother, leaving Artos out, as his father usually did, but in extension, those promises were also made to his whole House and their Province.

Artos had made his decision three years ago, during that week at the capital; he would not let his age or the timing of his birth in the family stop him from reaching the heights he knew he could achieve. He decided he would do whatever he had to in order to raise his station in life and, like it or not, the parts were all in motion now.

# Chapter Seven

Bakar and Tigran stood side by side as they waited with their horses for the barracks gates to open. At last they heard the latch lift from the inside and a voice cry out.

"Hark! Who dares to disturb the lair of evil king Babandur?"

"Very funny, Babandur!" called back Bakar.

He looked at Tigran and rolled his eyes as muffled snickers rose up from behind the gate.

"What's the secret password?" came another voice from inside the gate. It was Merak, the youngest of their group of friends.

"Gentleman," called out Prince Tigran, who was also grinning now. "If you don't let us in at once, I shall refuse to tell you all about my extraordinary meeting with the King of Kings!"

"Ah, then you shall wait all day!" retorted Babandur. "We aren't interested in the tedium of Parthian politics. Now then, the secret password?"

Bakar waited for the laughter to die down before speaking. "Perhaps you don't want to hear about old Mithridates, but if you don't let us in, we won't be able to recount how your Prince Tigran killed an assassin in the dead of night with nothing but his bare hands and a clay lantern."

The young men on the other side couldn't open the gate fast enough.

It was nearly four weeks now since Tigran and Bakar had left Ecbatana, and the terror of the assassination attempt was beginning to fade into something more resembling a heroic tale of adventure. Bakar hadn't forgotten the severity of the situation, but their return home had been peaceful and, now that they were back at the barracks of the Royal Guard, the danger seemed very far away indeed.

Bakar looked up at Babandur's tree trunk of an arm as the gate swung open. Babandur and Merak greeted the travelers exuberantly, and Bakar was happy to be back among his friends.

Babandur was the same age as Tigran, although much taller and stronger than all of them, and always seemed to find his way into trouble with Captain Harat, but he was a formidable fighter, more so even than Prince Tigran. During training rounds, Bakar once witnessed Babandur singlehandedly take down three men twice as experienced as he. His talents in combat were already the stuff of myth and legend.

Standing next to Babandur, Merak looked hopelessly out of place, but the wide grin on his face revealed his affable nature and genuine pleasure at being among his friends. Merak was short and stout, not at all built for the life of a member of the Royal Guard. Had it not been for his cruel widowed mother's friendship with Tigran's father, Merak could never have found his home here in the Royal Guard. Bakar felt a kinship with Merak, though it was something of which they never spoke. Abandoned by their mothers, the two of them had found family and brotherhood amidst the rigors of life in the Royal Guard.

"Now then, what of this assassin?" asked Babandur, who turned his broad shoulders toward Tigran and placed his large, scarred hands on the Prince's shoulders. "What was he after? Were you wounded?"

"A superficial wound from a dagger," said the Prince casually, "nothing serious."

"We don't know why it happened," Bakar added, "but it was clear this man was out for Tigran's blood. We don't know who he was or who sent him."

"A true mystery," Merak said with fascination.

"His barbaric appearance and small stature belied his skill," said Tigran. "When I first saw him, I expected a trivial fight. Now I understand why Captain Harat has always cautioned us against making assumptions about our opponents."

"But what would anyone stand to gain with you dead?" asked Merak.

"If only we knew," Bakar replied.

"Well, one thing is for certain; whatever they wanted, it couldn't be to replace you on your ever-so-exciting journey to the bowels of the Parthian Empire," said Babandur with a theatrical yawn.

"You're just jealous!" said Tigran with a spirited scoff. "If I recall, Captain Harat banned you and Aro from Ecbatana after a certain incident with that ale merchant's twin daughters, did he not?"

"I'll tell you this, my Prince," Babandur said, "it was well worth it!"

"But where is Aro, anyway," Bakar asked, realizing only then that the last of their group was not there. "He will be disappointed to have missed the telling of Tigran's battle."

"Aro is off doing what he does best," said Merak. "He was sent out with some noblemen, to lead a hunting expedition out west."

Babandur grimaced. "Sounds incredibly boring, if you ask me. I was relieved that he volunteered so I didn't have to."

"But you know Aro," Merak laughed, "he'll take any chance he can get to be on a horse and wander off to shoot some arrows."

"So, Tigran, did anything *else* happen on your journey to Ecbatana?" asked Babandur with a smirk.

"Wh - What do you mean?" Tigran asked, his complexion turning an

almost imperceptible shade of pink. His reaction made Bakar wonder again about those several occasions he helped the Prince sneak off in the night without Harat's consent. He had his suspicions about what was going on, but Tigran wasn't ordinarily so secretive, so Bakar hadn't said anything about it either. Whatever it was, he hoped it didn't mean Parthia's grip on the Prince's heart was tightening.

Before Babandur could press further, a messenger arrived to summon the Prince to the King's court for an audience with his uncle, the King. As Tigran bid his friends a hasty farewell, Bakar couldn't help but wonder if he would ever learn the answer to Babandur's question.

———•–••–•———

Prince Tigran's father paced the floor and snorted several furious breaths. "Artavazd, it's only a few more horses a year. I'm not entirely sure this increase in tribute merits such an impassioned fit on the part of the King of Armenia."

King Artavazd took a long look at his brother through glossy, sunken eyes. He had lived longer than many ever expected, and he was tired – but he still had strength enough to defend his homeland from the likes of his greedy brother.

"I might agree with you, brother, were it not for the disease that just last month swept through our kingdom's best stables," he replied wearily. "And every year thus far they have asked for *a few more horses*."

He coughed at length, his breath rasping ragged in his lungs. It was as though every altercation with his brother aged him an additional ten years. His haggard face showed every battle of wits, every shouting match, every unfortunate betrayal.

The Crowned Prince waited until his coughing fit subsided before continuing.

"Look, I know it won't be easy to sacrifice that number of horses, but tributes are the price we must pay to be afforded the protection of the Empire."

"Protection?" said the King with a scoff that elicited yet more coughing. Several moments passed again before he was able to continue,

"And how are we supposed to keep our silver, copper and tin mines operating at full capacity without more horses? What about the profits we stand to lose? What protection does *that* afford us?"

"Does King Mithridates not provide protection and security for commerce? Remember, brother, it was you who agreed to pay tribute to the Empire for these very reasons."

"I agreed because you convinced most of the council members of either an impending attack the likes of which would reduce our homeland to rubble, or a bleak future of complete financial ruin –" his mind lingered over the memory of those days, and he struggled to find words that might hope to carry weight with his brother's opinion, "an attack, coincidentally, that never occurred. But now our nobility has split into opposing factions, which is destroying the stability and unity that was our father's life's work. The cost of your *protection* is making our Kingdom weaker."

Crowned Prince Tigran crossed his arms angrily. "Does he not allow our nobles to keep their rule and collect their taxes and make their own profits as they see fit?"

"For the most part," replied Artavazd with a withered sneer. "Meanwhile, our nobility is at the mercy of the Parthian throne while our own coffers quickly empty. My dear brother, the only protection paying tribute now affords us is from incurring Parthia's wrath for failing to pay it."

Tigran took a step closer. When he spoke, his voice was lower, but the seriousness in his tone was elevated.

"We don't have a choice but to do what Parthia asks of us. As you said, our country is not united enough to dare oppose the might of the Empire. Our nobles in the south and eastern borders do well with their trade agreements; they would be fools to offer up their cavalry units against the King of Kings. To say nothing of the barbarians roaming free in our Highlands to the north; while we were busy wasting blood in a doomed battle with Parthia, they would be organizing to loot our cities."

Artavazd rubbed his hands in frustration over his yellow, hollowed cheeks. His lungs felt as if they were on fire.

"You know I am working to unite the warring Highland tribes."

Artavazd could see that Tigran was about to begin another tirade, but he raised his hand in a plea for silence.

"Once we have accomplished that goal, our valiant country will once again be more self-sufficient. There are still much unexploited resources to the north. When our father succeeded in uniting Armenia, our nation's capital was built at last. It was built here in the North region, because that is where the true power of our kingdom is. Greed had not yet embittered the hearts of our noble houses in those days. Our nation was united in a common cause. Armenia can be that way again."

"Brother, I fear your senility is clouding your faculties," said Tigran with unabashed concern. "You make it sound as though uniting the Highlanders is as easy as gifting them a few chickens and asking them to please get along. They will never pay the Royal taxes as other provinces do, they can never be civilized enough to attend council meetings."

Tigran then held his hands behind his back, staring down as he paced in front of Artavazd. Finally, he spoke.

"I wonder why you are fighting so hard for an Armenia that no longer exists. Could it be, perhaps, because Parthia is not the one to blame for the fall of our beloved homeland, after all?"

The King closed his eyes and sat back in his throne. He took a few slow, laboring breaths before lifting a cup of ale to his mouth with a quavering hand. The liquid did nothing to help his blistering throat. He replaced the cup and looked directly at his younger brother through eyes that were failing, but which had seen much in their many years.

"I may be old, brother, but my faculties do not fail me. The only thing we gain by paying tribute to Parthia is an indebtedness that they have manufactured. We become pawns in their plot to conquer the world even as we bleed ourselves dry of resources. To be sure, I am a very old man, but I am still the King of Armenia and, as long as I remain King, I will work to reunite *all* our lands and the rest of the Provinces. Armenia's sovereignty is at very dire risk, even if you don't see it. A united country will give us the way out – and I know exactly how to make it happen."

"You stubborn fool," shouted Tigran, "You threatened to kill our trade and with it our industries and economy! Your senseless pride keeps you from admitting that Parthia is much stronger and wealthier than us, and like it or not, we will always be at their mercy. You have spilled the blood of our brothers in your relentless pursuit of independence from an Empire that offers Armenia a path into the future! If anything will bring about the ultimate death of Armenia, old man, I can assure you it is not the King of Kings."

The voice of the King's younger brother was shrill and echoed disagreeably off the stone walls.

"Father, what are you shouting about?"

Young Prince Tigran stood at the doorway, wide-eyed.

King Artavazd and the Prince's father turned toward young Prince Tigran. The King sighed; it wouldn't matter that his ill-tempered brother opposed him so vehemently, were it not for the effect it was having on the Prince. Artavazd was doing everything in his power to nurture the qualities in his bright nephew that made him such a natural leader, and he was aware that Captain Harat was doing so as well. Unfortunately, it seemed that his father's influence was winning out more every day – but if the boy wouldn't take up the fight for Armenia after he and the Captain were gone, who would?

It was a question whose answer the King could not bear to contemplate.

———•—•••—•———

"I am happy that you have returned safely, young Tigran, now tell me about this attempt on your life en route to Parthia." King Artavazd's feeble voice wavered with concern.

"Yes, Uncle," replied Prince Tigran. His uncle looked weaker every time Tigran saw him.

"And why am I hearing of this just now?" broke in his father, "did that obviously lacking Captain of yours think to tell *me*? No!" Then his features softened a bit, and he added, "Although, of course, I am relieved to see you are safe, my son."

"Am I to understand that my dearest uncle and beloved father are arguing over the Parthian tribute?" inquired the Prince, eager to change the subject. He felt sorry for his uncle the King. Although Artavazd was undoubtedly a wise ruler, Tigran often felt as though the man was past his prime. He loved his uncle, but it was no secret that the King opposed his father's growing loyalties to Parthia, not to mention his own.

The Prince's father scowled. "Young man, have you ever stopped to consider that he is your 'dearest uncle' only because all of your other uncles were sent to their deaths in ill-advised, ill-fated battles against Parthia?"

Prince Tigran realized his father was in one of his particularly ferocious moods. He raised his hands in a gesture of appeasement.

"All right, can we please have a civilized discussion about this? As you know, I was honored with an audience by King Mithridates in Ecbatana. I have learned much about the King of Kings and his intentions toward Armenia."

"Oh?" said King Artavazd, who seemed less than enthusiastic about the news. "What did you learn, my boy?"

"As far as I understood, Mithridates wants nothing more than the various lands within his empire to simply coexist peaceably and function cohesively, for the benefit of all," said the Prince, proud to be discussing matters of politics with the two most influential men in his kingdom.

"You know, the Empire as a whole seems to be not much different from our own kingdom," he said, "though on a much larger scale of course. In their case, what are our provinces, for them, would be other kingdoms. The King of Kings worries about the same things we worry about; in-fighting, civil unrest, tax-collecting, threats to the Crown..."

"What sort of threats?" asked the King.

"As a matter of fact, there seem to be a number of dangers from within his own family," said Prince Tigran. "While I was there, there was an incident involving a relative acting as a spy. The King explained to me that it was one of the frequent attempts to unseat him from power. Apparently it's something that requires his ongoing attention."

King Artavazd nodded thoughtfully, but the Prince could see his speech did not sway him in the slightest. He sympathized with his uncle. Part of him truly envied the depth of his loyalty to their homeland – Bakar and Captain Harat were so like him in that respect – yet he couldn't help but feel that the old King was unnecessarily protective, perhaps even to the detriment of the kingdom he so loved.

"You know, Uncle," continued the Prince, "I understand your reticence to embrace becoming part of the Parthian Empire, but many of the countries that have chosen to cooperate with Mithridates have enjoyed much growth and prosperity. Perhaps it would not be as difficult to pay tribute if we were not expending so much of our energy and resources railing against the Empire."

"My son, you are wise beyond your years," said the Prince's father, with an arrogant grin in the direction of the throne. He walked over to Tigran and put his arm around his shoulders. "Brother, you would do well to listen to the wisdom of this young man, whom you have so diligently mentored these nearly twenty years."

Even as Tigran nodded in agreement, he knew that he and his father were not after a closer alliance with Parthia for the same reasons. His father was neither a fighter nor a leader; he was a trader and negotiator at heart who simply saw the move in terms of the coins it would put in his coffers, and the coffers of those allies he had turned to his side.

The Prince had seen little of his father as a boy, and he realized that this display of paternal love was more about him getting what he wanted than genuine pride in his only son. Still, it made sense for Tigran to side with his father now; Parthia offered more opportunities for political advancement in Tigran's own life – and of course, there was Roya...

"There are other ways to cultivate a prosperous and peaceful country," mumbled the King, clearly crestfallen at the father-and-son alliance that stood before him. He took a long sip of water that spilled slightly onto his wiry gray beard. He cursed under his breath and did his best to mop up the mess with a corner of his robes. Tigran observed his father rolling his eyes at the spectacle.

At last, King Artavazd looked up at his brother and his nephew. "You may not agree with me," he began, "but one of the fortunate aspects of kingship is that I am not required to obtain your blessing before I make decisions. For now, we *will* try to make peace with the Highlanders. We will also be ceasing negotiations of new trade agreements with Parthian enterprises, in the interest of spurring our own self-sufficiency. Finally, next summer, our tributes will be the same as I agreed to initially: not even a single additional hair from our fine Caspian horses will I gift to that viper you two like to call 'the King of Kings.'"

Prince Tigran wasn't sure how to reply; he didn't dare tell his uncle that he couldn't imagine what Mithridates would do once he learned of Armenia's disobedience. He stood there, wide-eyed, then began, "Uncle, I am hesitant to – "

"No, that's enough for now," sighed the King. "I am tired. Leave me to rest."

# Chapter Eight

Captain Harat steadily ascended the steps leading up to the Royal Residence. He ignored his old, protesting knees, and tried to keep his breathing steady. Nonetheless, he was in pain and out of breath by the time he reached the outer doors of the King's Chamber. Two weeks had passed since their return from Parthia and his first report to the King, but now the King asked for him today. So, here he was.

Harat nodded at the guard standing outside, who rapped on the door. The eunuch Theo opened it from the inside with a warming smile. Theo had been the Royal Houses' head servant since well before Captain Harat's bones ever began aching. As a House servant, he was required to be loyal to the Crown, but through the years, Harat found Theo to be genuinely and immensely loyal to King Artavazd, and that was why he trusted him.

"Good Day, Captain," the eunuch said, "it is always good to see you. Please enter, the King is awaiting your visit."

"Thank you, Theo," Harat replied as he walked in.

Theo walked out and closed the door behind him. Harat marched across the room toward a couch upon which a bundle of blankets was moving about. He could hear the King's wheezing breath as he neared.

"Theo, is that you? Where is the Captain? I thought he was coming." King Artavazd said, turning his head from left to right.

"I am here, my King, it is I," Harat replied, trying to hide the pity in his voice. This wise and strong King who had vehemently held back the military aggressions fostered by Parthia for all those years was now facing his last battle...but the battle of mortality was one nobody could win. He would sooner or later join his ancestors in the afterlife. Harat could not ignore the fact that he wasn't too far behind now himself.

*If you Gods have any pity on me, you will let me join my ancestors before I fall into such a state as the one the King now suffers.*

"Captain Harat, I am pleased you came," the King said.

"Of course, my King,"

The King tried to pull himself up and fell into a coughing fit. Harat leaned in and helped him, putting a cloth in his weak grip to wipe his mouth.

"Thank you Harat," the King spoke between breaths, "I know I am dying, but the Gods don't see fit to take me yet. I do not know why; perhaps they think I have not suffered enough in this life," he let out a laugh, and it quickly turned into another coughing episode.

"They do not want to sadden the world by taking you too soon," Harat said softly, and with deep reverence.

The Captain had served King Artavazd all his adult life, and admired and respected him greatly. He couldn't help but wonder what would come of all they had fought for when the Gods finally *did* take the King.

The King snickered and replied, "I fear there are not many still left alive but you that might be upset with my passing."

"Forgive me, but that is not true my King; there is a whole new generation of boys that have grown to men knowing their King cares for them."

The King waved away the Captain's pleasantries and motioned for Harat to sit beside him.

"Let us not waste any more time, for it is not something either of us have in abundance," the King began. "We both know there are at least as many, if not more, of our citizens that would have me and my policies gone. During the years we were busy holding back the invading armies, my brother and our Ambassador were slowly turning our nobles against us. Perhaps there was something more I could have done to stop it, but if I had, the situation may have gotten worse. It is not something I have the luxury of dwelling on."

As if to press the point, the King fell into another outburst of coughing.

Harat softly rested a hand on the Kings back, holding in check the shock of how frail he felt beneath his fingers. He waited patiently for the King to recover.

"We cannot," the King finally began to say before pausing again for a gulp of air, "we cannot trust the loyalties of many of the lords from our southern and eastern provinces."

"Their loyalties are as fickle as a feather in the wind," Harat conceded, "but there are still many houses in the west and north that are strongly loyal to Armenia, and stand staunchly against the Parthian intrusions."

The King looked up at Harat with sullen eyes.

"That is correct, my wise old friend, the northern provinces depend very little on the more popular trade routes that pass from east to west. Sure, they are crude, stubborn, and some say less civilized than most, but they are also more self-reliant, and are far removed from the temptations of greed, unlike many of our other lords and citizens."

The King coughed again, and Harat spied a spot of blood on the cloth in his hand.

"I have been trying to put the pieces in place up North, pieces that will ensure the Northern regions will help keep our Kingdom from breaking apart."

"Then please, my King, instruct me on how I can help you in this cause," Harat quickly said.

"I am afraid this battle will not be yours," the King replied, "I plan on unifying the Highlander tribes and formally bringing both them and the lands they roam back into the Kingdom."

Captain Harat's brows rose in surprise at this declaration. The King knew Harat had no love for the Highlanders; rebels that refused to pay tax or tribute to the Royal House, horsemen who lived in scattered villages in the harsh mountain lands, tribesmen who often feuded amongst themselves; a people who, in times of strife, raided nearby towns and villages and anyone else they came across.

"I, but how, they -" Harat's words stumbled out as he tried to reply.

"They deserve their own lands, lands that still have resources that have gone unnoticed," the King said with conviction. "But more importantly, they themselves are a resource. They are horsemen, fighters, survivors, they are the missing component that will make us strong again in all ways."

Harat thought on it for a moment, if for nothing else but the King's benefit. Though they seldom disagreed, Harat had always spoken his mind with the King and so he found himself asking, "You mean to make nobles of the mountain men? How will that be possible if everything they stand for is at odds with the rest of the Kingdom, against the very idea of nobility itself?"

The King waved his frail arm again.

"Bah, what is that but a word? Do they not have their own *nobles*; their chieftains and tribal elders that advise, lead and protect their people? They may not be so detached from the rest of the Kingdom if we invite them in again."

"So you will give them their own province?"

"Two provinces, in fact. Eventually," the King replied quickly. "I believe we can add two new and distinct provinces along our wild northern boarders without much disruption. But that will likely still be years away. For now, we have to gently remind them that they are part of the Kingdom, and put them on the path of uniting themselves."

"My King," Harat said without thought, "you know I will do what I must to -"

"I know, my friend," the King cut in, "but this task must be put upon those who will still be around to benefit from the outcome. I will be asking our young Prince Tigran to take the lead on perhaps this last request of mine."

"You know the boy won't refuse you," Harat said, not hiding the worry in his tone. "It will be a very dangerous mission; how can you trust -"

Again, the King cut him off; "I am not ignorant of the fact that it will be dangerous," he said, a hint of anger in his raspy voice now. "Do you think I enjoy sending my own nephew into harm's way? But he is a man now, and he will be the Crowned Prince soon enough, and if the Gods are merciful, he will be King not soon after. He must know his people, all his people. And it must start now."

It was obvious that the King had already thought long and hard on this, and Captain Harat quickly realized there was no changing his mind on the matter.

"As you wish, my King, I am sure Prince Tigran will not disappoint you," Harat said.

"Let us hope not, my old friend," the King replied. "Now then; a Northern Lord has helped me foster a tentative negotiation with a tribe that is willing to hear us out. I have been told their new leader, a man called Vahan, is an honorable man who will keep his word. Prince Tigran will lead a small contingent of guardsmen up north to meet with him."

Harat did not like this idea at all; he did not have as much faith in those tribes as the King did, for he had fought them in days past and was aware just how ruthless they could be.

"As you say, my King," Harat forced himself to say. "I will prepare the supplies myself and put up my best men for the escort."

The King gazed back at Harat with a disappointing look. "Let's wait until *after* I speak to the Prince...And perhaps we should let *him* pick the guardsmen for the journey. After all, we want the Prince to understand he is needed. He is old enough and trained enough now, we must begin building his confidence in himself."

"Correct again of course, my King," Harat said. "And I am confident the Prince will not fail us."

Then the King let out his breath and sunk further into the couch. For a moment Harat feared the worst, but then he saw the King move again, and he was able to let out his own breath in relief.

Harat struggled to hear the King's next words; "Let us hope he doesn't, my old friend...need to rest now."

The Captain lowered his King in a prone position on the couch and covered him with a bear fur blanket.

*Let us hope he doesn't, my old friend*, Harat echoed in his mind.

———•———•——

Nearly three weeks had passed since the Crowned Prince's loud and frenzied footfalls had reverberated in the corridor leading to Artavazd's private chambers. But today, the elder Tigran burst through the King's door, ready to rekindle a shouting match, but was stayed by the sight before him. His ailing fool of a brother was coughing so violently he appeared to be choking to death. The boy was at his side, pouring him a cup of fresh water. He looked up, seeming startled by his father's abrupt intrusion.

"Father, you have returned. But what is the matter?" his son asked while handing the cup to his uncle.

"I might ask you the same thing, boy!" Tigran cried out. "How do you expect a father to feel when he comes home from a business trip sanctioned by His Highness, only to discover a plot has been unfolding behind his back, a plot to send his only son to certain death?"

"Father – "

Enraged as the elder Tigran was, it seemed inappropriate to continue his verbal assault while his brother's jagged coughs looked to be tearing his last breaths painfully from his body. He crossed his arms and fidgeted impatiently until, at last, Artavazd' coughing fit subsided.

"Well, Brother, what say you?" he bellowed when it was done. "Am I to understand that, at your request, my son is to be leading a mission to the Highlands as a diplomatic envoy?"

The King took a small sip of water and cleared his throat. "You understand perfectly, brother."

"You send me away on business only to order my son to take up this insane, suicidal crusade of yours behind my back?" shouted Tigran.

"It was not an order; it was merely a request," Artavazd managed to say before the coughing struck him yet again. He covered his mouth with his robes and wheezed for air between each painful cough.

"And *you*, young man," Tigran said, turning to his son, "I cannot understand how you would ever agree to such a dangerous and futile 'request.' Just three weeks ago we stood in this very room and agreed that an alliance with Parthia was best for our kingdom – and now you are siding with your misaligned old uncle on this crazy quest? And with winter approaching, no less!"

"Father, it's a short enough mission that we will be back before winter begins, and it is important to my uncle, our King. It means much to him – " the Prince lowered his voice so that his father strained to hear him over the ceaseless coughing, " – especially in his current condition. And moreover, I am excited about the opportunity and the confidence the King puts in me. And I believe I can be successful in this. I can take care of myself, and this does not change how I feel about the Empire."

The elder Tigran boiled with ire. His son seemed to understand the value in Parthia and the uselessness of his brother, a King with one foot in the grave, so why was he choosing to undertake this mission?

"Need I remind you that those Highland tribes do not recognize the ruling family? In the past they have shown no discretion when it comes to attacking outsiders that venture into their territory, especially when those outsiders are there to demand capitulation."

Between sputtering coughs the King cut in, "Ah, brother, do I have more faith in your son than you?"

"Don't be ridiculous," Tigran said, "but what do those savages know about diplomacy? If I didn't know better, I'd swear you were trying to get my only son killed with this absurd task."

"I only asked, and he accepted," the King reiterated as his coughing attack subsided once again. He wiped his mouth and took a small sip of the water. "My nephew is a man now; it is his right to choose as he sees fit."

"Father," interjected the Prince, "it is true that I chose to accept this mission of my own free will. There was no coercion from Uncle."

"Your son wants to make his mark in life," Artavazd added. "I cannot deny him that noble endeavor, but I will not encourage him to do it elsewhere. If the boy wants to prove his worth, let him do so in his homeland."

Tigran wasn't sure what else to say about this most unwelcome development. His brother's inane rulings would no longer threaten Armenia's entry into the Empire once the King was laid to rest – which now seemed to be merely a matter of weeks away. Tigran could only hope that the damage Artavazd was doing now could be undone once the inevitable came to pass.

"This is utterly absurd," Tigran continued his protest, "winter will soon be upon us. I don't like any part of this ridiculous plan."

"Do not fear for my safety," his son replied, "if I leave at once and hurry up to the Highlands, my convoy should be back before we see any really heavy snowfall. I assure you, Father, this is a mission I am willing and eager to undertake, and I promise to return to you intact."

"But the ramifications if you succeed..." murmured the Prince's father before stopping himself.

The King's coughing fit flared up at the same moment and he felt assured that neither his son nor his brother had heard him. Tigran groaned crossly; all that could be done for now was to wait for his obstinate relic of a brother to die, and hope that his son returned alive.

# Chapter Nine

Prince Tigran awoke especially early on the day they were to leave, and was now walking among the horses and pack animals, surveying their supplies. The morning was perfect for a departure north; it was not yet unbearably cold and the ground was dry; though he would prefer to be heading back south to Ecbatana. This was the best he could hope for, at least for now.

Aro followed behind him. "I believe the caravan is ready," he said, "and I must confess I am more than ready for a healthy dose of adventure. Let us hope this mild weather is not an omen of an entirely uneventful journey."

The Prince smiled. His friend Aro was a model pupil of the Royal Guard, diligent in his training and ever eager to flex his considerable skill with a bow and arrow. Their friendship was founded on frankness; it was something that, for reasons Tigran couldn't quite name, he couldn't always manage with Bakar or any of his other friends.

"Fear not, Aro," replied the Prince. "We are headed where the winds whip the landscape into submission, to a region where you know we will not be welcome. The Highlander ruffians will ensure there is plenty of adventure to go around for us all."

"Are Merak and Babandur angry that you did not choose them to come?" Aro asked.

"Merak was relieved. As you know, he doesn't like riding horses for long periods of time, let alone venturing into hostile mountains," Tigran replied, "Babandur was, of course upset, but I could not take a chance on his volatile personality on this first, important meeting."

Tigran patted his horse's soft muzzle. Although it was true that he had agreed to undertake this journey for the sake of his uncle, he couldn't help but wish his mission had more to do with Parthia, or at the very least, that it would bring him closer to Roya, not farther away. Still, the King of Kings had made mention that the ability to gain the trust of one's subjects was an essential quality in a leader. It was possible that this mission would help to prove his worth, not just to the Armenian kingdom, but to the Empire as well. The thought heartened him.

Tigran could feel Aro watching him thoughtfully. "You're right, though, Aro, everything is ready. Once Bakar arrives, let's set off."

"You know," Aro remarked, "even if you aren't as excited as I to be heading up to the Highlands, surely you must be looking forward to your first real mission for the kingdom – you know, as leader."

"Of course," the Prince replied, "I admit I am weary of being a figurehead, though I do hope the gods will protect us and counsel me in my decision-making. My outcomes will be scrutinized carefully, and hopefully not only by my uncle."

"Ah yes, I have observed your fondness for the Parthian Empire," said Aro.

Tigran was alarmed; it was as though Aro was reading his thoughts. The Prince was about to protest, but his friend continued. "...and I can understand how it could entice you. I myself have a weakness for novelty and excitement, as you well know; but we have to ask ourselves what we truly want."

"Well, there is adventure to be had at home," Tigran admitted, "but if I am to speak plainly, friend to friend, adventurer to adventurer, Parthia indeed stirs my soul."

"Naturally, you'd have to be half dead for it not to. But even though I seek excitement at nearly every turn, for myself I would not want to live the life of a Parthian city dweller; filthy, crowded cities, streets filled with beggars who want and aristocrats who won't give, deceit and deception... it would be a loss of freedom I simply could not tolerate. I would feel trapped like an animal," said Aro. "Our kingdom is not dominated by such cities with buildings so crowded together they conceal the blue of the sky, roads that charge taxes and tolls to walk upon, while being open to the scrutiny of soldiers from the Empire at any time. Instead, ours is a Kingdom blessed by expanses of land rich with resources, where the Provinces still have enough room for commoners to hunt in open lands without seeing another for days; where your horse can freely gallop across wide-open plains and around mountains higher than the clouds. In a kingdom like ours, you know you are truly free."

Tigran smiled at his friend and then bowed his head, conflicted. "Is it that obvious how I feel?"

Aro's face broadened with a sly grin. "Almost as obvious as your secret tryst with that Parthian girl."

The Prince's eyes widened. "By the gods, you know about that, too?"

Aro laughed. "Indeed, and do not think I am the only one. My friend, you are a man who wears his heart on his sleeve."

Tigran wasn't sure how to respond. How could he not have known until this moment that his feelings toward Parthia were as plain as day? Sure, Parthia beckoned, but he hoped others could see that his loyalty to the Armenian throne was at least genuine. Maybe it wasn't as deep or as obvious as his uncle's, or Bakar's, or Harat's or even Aro's, but his loyalty was sincere enough. The proof was in the mission upon which they were about to embark, was it not? Still, he could not help but feel guilty.

Aro put a reassuring hand on his friend's shoulder.

"You have plenty of time to ruminate upon the future, Tigran. One thing I *do* know is that it's best to focus on the task at hand. Whether you're riding through a treacherous pass, negotiating with a hostile tribe, or even taking a piss, we must do our utmost to see our current obligation through before we can think on another one."

"You are correct of course," Tigran said, "now let's go see what is taking Bakar and the rest of the men so long. I'll not have them thinking I will be easy on them on my first day."

———•—••—•———

There was no doubt that the mission to the Highlands was going to be frigid. While the worst of the snowstorms hadn't yet befallen the kingdom this season, Bakar was still dreading the sharp mountain cold. He was placing the last of his warmest tunics in his satchel when Captain Harat entered the barracks.

"It is time to go, Bakar," said the Captain, rubbing his hands together for warmth. "I am sure Prince Tigran and the rest of the group is waiting on you."

"Will you come to wish us all luck before we depart?" asked Bakar.

"No," replied Harat, his voice even more gruff than usual, "it is Tigran's job now to rally the men."

Bakar was surprised when he'd learned that King Artavazd had commanded Harat not to accompany Tigran on his mission. He guessed it was because of the Captain's open disdain for the Highland tribes. Still, Bakar could understand the Captain's worry, this was the first mission Tigran would be leading without Harat's protection – and the Highlanders were not exactly known for their docile ways. This was no minor first step to be undertaking alone.

"Well," said Bakar, slinging his satchel over his back, "I'm off, then."

"Wait, Bakar," interjected the Captain. "Just because I will not be there does not mean you and the others can behave like halfwit children when their father's back is turned. You are old enough and wise enough now to officially be in the Royal Guard. I expect to hear nothing but accounts of your exemplary conduct upon your safe return."

Bakar had to shut his mouth to keep it from dropping open. So many of his friends had been inducted into the Royal Guard well before him – except for Merak, who had always been smaller, younger, slower, and forever a step behind. He could not ignore the honor Harat bestowed upon him now, despite his harsh words.

"Yes, Captain," he managed, straightening up a little and trying to conceal a prideful smile.

"The Prince is in charge," continued Harat sternly, "but you must see to it that his attentions are not diverted. Thank the gods that Tigran decided to leave behind Merak and Babandur, that rabble-rouser."

"Likely a wise choice," agreed Bakar, who hoped to placate the Captain in some small way before their departure, "although Prince Tigran has profited greatly from your instruction. We all have. Your guidance and training have kept Tigran from peril before; I am sure it will do so this time as well. Besides, according to King Artavazd, the new leader of the Highland tribes is an honorable chieftain."

The Captain shook his head. "Meeting this 'honorable chieftain' and getting him to do as the King wishes are two different beasts entirely. It would be unwise to underestimate the inherent dangers in an expedition such as this."

"Yes, Captain," replied Bakar. He paused a moment to choose his next words carefully. "...But these are the same tribes who once held King Artavazd's father, Artashes the Good, in such high esteem. I don't believe Tigran is tasked with forcing the Highlanders to do as the King desires, but rather to attempt to rekindle the sense of fidelity they once felt for the Crown."

Harat's frown turned around and he put his strong hand on his pupil's shoulder.

"Bakar, you are very wise for your age; that is why you will watch the Prince's back in ways the others cannot. There is no one else I trust. I will not be there...and there will come a day when having me there is no longer an option at all. You are no longer boys, but men..." Harat's eyes were filled with pride.

"Yes Captain, of course I – "

"That's enough of this now," Harat fiercely cut him off, his tone suddenly hardening up once again. "Your prince is waiting."

# Chapter Ten

In the winter, the North lands were all at once magnificent and forbidding. The sheer mountain passes through which Tigran's small contingent traveled were covered with ice and snow. In the springtime, when green forests and songbirds softened the jagged landscape, the region appeared almost welcoming to outsiders. Now, the bare mountainsides and whipping wind made it clear that they must earn every step of progress they intended to make.

The group had been journeying north-by-west from the Armenian capital, Artashat, for five days now and there was already more snow than Tigran expected. The expanse of whiteness demanded a hushed reverence as they traveled. It also meant they must be much more careful where they stepped, especially now, as they traveled up a sheer, pitiless mountainside. The group made long, tight zigzags upward, their pace slow and cautious. At times the terrain was so steep that they traveled among the tops of trees whose trunks they had passed on their path below. Luckily Armenia's famous, surefooted Caspian horses were renowned to excel in this type of terrain. Shorter than other horses, with a slim body and graceful neck, people were often surprised by just how strong and extremely hardy they were. The horses sloping shoulders, straight back, and strong, stout legs - with oval shaped hoofs that more resembled that of an ass – made them the ideal steed in these mountain regions, where they naturally roamed.

For the last three days, since passing through the last Northern town, a small village called Tasha, they had not seen one trace of civilization.

At the beginning of this journey the sky had been a crisp blue; now, it too was as white as the untouched snows. When the wind stirred the snow underfoot it became impossible to tell where the white-capped mountaintops ended and the sky began. The scene was in every way the antithesis of his last journey away from the Capital, to Parthia. Ecbatana was warm and vibrant, buzzing with life and promise. These bleak, harsh lands promised him nothing but a harrowing mission through freezing mountains, every day colder than the last.

Tigran's thoughts turned to Roya. When he closed his eyes he could still see how she looked that first night, her crimson dress and inky black hair kissed by the glow of candlelight. He could still feel the tenderness of her touch, how she had pressed into him, wanting. Tigran had stolen as many moments as possible away from his official business in Ecbatana to be with Roya, but it hadn't been enough. When she left his arms that last day, behind the crumbling old temple, she'd taken a piece of his soul with her.

The winds picked up again and lashed themselves against Tigran's face, which was already stinging from the cold. These unforgiving Highlands held no charm at all next to the warm, tender sanctuary of Roya's embrace.

So far, Tigran's first mission as commander was passing without incident. Bakar and Aro were most welcome companions; it was reassuring to know that they, along with eight of the Royal Guard's most experienced men, were traveling with him. The group was small enough to not be misinterpreted as an arrival of force, but large enough and skilled enough to hopefully protect them, if the need arose. The men complained little about the harsh travel conditions; in their lifetimes, most of them had already endured countless wind-whipped, bitterly cold journeys. Tigran was grateful for their experience.

Just as the men reached a narrow plateau in their ascent, the winds grew still. Around them the large, bare trees were thick enough to hinder both the wind and sight of the path onward. The wind's sudden calmness made Tigran realize he had been listening to it whistle in his ears nearly the entire time; if the landscape was hushed before, it was doubly so now. The horses' ears pricked and Tigran's men looked about themselves uneasily. All the Prince could hear now was the icy mountain air moving in and out of his lungs.

The stillness was shattered by a piercing cry from the eldest of the guardsmen. Tigran and the others turned just in time to see the man grip an arrow that sliced into his neck. The guardsman looked back at his companions with horror and confusion in his eyes. With the arrow still in his trembling fist, he tried to speak, but in place of words, a torrent of blood surged from his lips. His eyes widened in panic just before his muscles gave way and he toppled from his horse, dead.

Then, out of everywhere and nowhere at once, more arrows began to whiz past, just over their heads.

"Sire, an ambush!" cried Aro.

In an instant, two more guardsmen and four of their horses were downed. The remaining men moved to form a protective half-circle about the Prince. As Tigran crouched behind, unsure of what to do and completely in shock, the unseen attackers continued their assault. Dozens of arrows sailed just above their heads, crisscrossing from virtually all angles.

Tigran watched the chaos through the slivers of space between the men. Just beyond this protective barrier lay three of his Royal Guard; men he'd been raised with, as brothers, impaled with arrows and bleeding to death. Tigran's chest heaved bitterly as more arrows flew overhead. Was this another attack on his life? Or simply the risk of crossing into these barbaric lands? Tigran was grateful for the protection the mountain afforded them on at least one side – but this situation seemed to be growing grimmer with each passing moment.

Suddenly, Bakar cried out. His horse dropped, sending Bakar falling backward into the semi-circle, next to the Prince. Tigran pulled him back away from his horse in a panic.

"Bakar! Your leg!" he exclaimed.

Before plunging into his horse's throat, an arrow had torn the leg of Bakar's trousers. Blood seeped from the long gash and was already well soaked through his garments. The horse lay in front of them, bleeding profusely and gasping for breath.

"The arrow only grazed me," reassured Bakar through gritted teeth.

"I am not gravely wounded."

"You will stay back here with me; you are not well enough to stand," Tigran demanded.

Tigran and Bakar looked up at the six remaining men crouching now before them. With the exception of Aro, all of them looked to be at a loss for what to do, bewitched by the maddening onslaught of arrows flying every which way. Aro, on the other hand, had an arrow loaded in his bow and was surveying their surroundings intently.

Bakar noticed, as well, and asked, "Is he looking for a target?"

"I don't know," replied Tigran. "How can he find his target in such a mess of arrows?"

The remaining guardsmen began to argue over what to do. Experience told them they were well outnumbered and that the Prince could not be protected in this manner indefinitely. Their panicked voices grew in intensity until they were shouting over one another.

"We should choose a direction and fight our way out!" one yelled.

"That's suicide!" cried another. "It would be safer to surrender."

"And surrender isn't suicide? Back the way we came is our best option," said a third.

"There are arrows coming from that direction as well!"

The men yelled over one another until their arguing was punctuated by another bloodcurdling shriek. A moment later the fifth man fell, his eye punctured by an arrow. The man grimaced and whimpered in pain as blood rushed from the wound. His chest heaved up and down and, looking directly at Tigran with his one remaining eye, he breathed his last.

"Tigran," whispered Bakar, "this is your mission. You have to make a decision. Quickly."

Tigran could only stare at the pain and gore of his fallen brothers. He tried to think, but a thundering in his ears clouded his thoughts.

He could order the remaining men to charge, but no matter which direction he chose, he'd be sending them headlong into a barrage of oncoming arrows. If he split them into two groups to make a run for it, they'd likely get themselves lost in this unfamiliar terrain, if they even survived the attackers. Harat had trained him well and hard, but the situation they faced now was beyond anything he could have ever prepared for. Tigran instinctively knew what to do when it was only him against the assassin all those weeks ago, but this was not the same; these men were under *his* command now, they were *his* responsibility... and they were his friends, falling dead around him; Tigran just couldn't see any way out of it.

"I cannot be decisive and say, Bakar, for danger and death lie in any command I could give," he said quietly.

"Sire." He heard Bakar urge again. "Do not try to think on it, choose what you feel is the best option."

Finally, he was about to make a decision when Aro put a hand on his shoulder to stay him.

"Sire, look at these new rounds of arrows now tracking from the south and east," said Aro, drawing a line across the sky with his free hand, "they are not firing at us, but over us, towards the north. Those who were firing at us first are there."

As Tigran followed Aro's gestures, the thundering in his ears began to subside and, indeed, it did appear that their small group was no longer getting hit. "Fire your arrows to those woods to our north!" Tigran ordered the remaining men, and they did so.

"I believe you are correct my friend," Tigran said to Aro, "now I only hope this other group does not fire upon us next."

"One problem at a time, remember?" Aro said, his eyes still closely scanning their surroundings. Suddenly he turned away from the Prince, readied an arrow, and fired it into the nearest trees north of them. A moment later, to everyone's surprise, a concealed archer in a far-off tree fell to the ground, dead. In the moments that followed, the few remaining arrows coming from the north faded to none, and the plateau was once again filled with an uneasy silence.

"It is over," said Aro as he lowered his bow.

"But what *was* it?" said Tigran. "Never in my life have I seen such a frenzy of arrows; such an ambush for only eleven men!"

"We are but six now," said Bakar, who was busy tying off his wound with a leather strap from his fallen horse's saddle, "but we must count our blessings. The gods have protected us and kept our Prince alive when

we were entirely outnumbered."

Tigran nodded, remorseful. "I should be dead, not these men."

Aro shook his head. "We are all members of the Royal Guard, Prince Tigran, sworn to protect you."

"And protect me you did, Aro – " said Tigran, "I owe my life to you, to all of you."

As Tigran spoke, he saw one guardsman, then another, turn their heads sharply in different directions. He was about to ask what was going on when he noticed some rustling in the trees out of the corner of his eye. A moment later, a dozen or so men emerged from the trees around them.

Tigran recognized them immediately as Highland Fighters. Most were on horseback; some were on foot. The Prince's men instinctively resumed their defensive position. Tigran saw Aro's fingers twitch, ready to raise his bow.

Tigran raised a hand, signaling his men not to fire.

"We thank you for the help," he said to the newcomers.

A friendly laugh emerged from one of them, then a man came forward and gestured to his fellow Highlanders to stand down. The man was tall, with long wild hair, and he walked toward Prince Tigran with a proud air about him. His weathered skin and toned musculature proclaimed him an outdoorsman, a fighter. As he approached, Tigran motioned for his men to stand down as well. Tigran's instincts told him that this man – whoever he was – did not mean to harm him, at least not now.

"You have had quite a welcome to our lands already, so I won't trouble myself to welcome you again," said the man with an affable smile. "I am Vahan, chieftain of the Tibareni tribe. Come, let us move away to friendlier ground."

———•—••—•———

On the advice of the chieftain Vahan, their group turned south toward the Tibareni village. It seemed they had found the right mountain, but they were on the wrong side. Bakar was atop one of their horses, which was lent to him since, indeed, he looked to be in no shape to walk yet. One of the tribesmen dressed his wound with a salve that had felt like molten stones upon his flesh, but it managed to seal the gash on his leg which, though minor in appearance, had persisted in bleeding until their intervention.

The tribesmen's horses were Caspians, like their own, but smaller, stockier, and even more sure-footed than the ones bred at the Capital. Bakar was all at once amazed by the strength and agility of such a comparatively small beast and pleased because the Tibareni's horse was effortless to handle through the narrow, steeply-pitched path and maze of trees.

Prince Tigran's battered group and the tribesmen made their way single file down a narrow mountain path from the plateau where they had been rescued. The path was well obscured by dense trees; Bakar felt sure if they were on their own, they would never have discovered it. Tigran and Vahan were at the front of their queue and, every time there was a bend in the path, Bakar could just see them up ahead. Though he was too far behind to hear what they were saying, the two seemed to be deep in amiable conversation. Bakar hoped Vahan was as friendly as he seemed.

Just in front of Bakar's horse was its handler, who made his way on foot. The tribesman hadn't said much at all during the last several hours, but Bakar was curious to learn more about the Tibareni. There was no doubt these men had saved their lives, but it didn't mean they were entirely trustworthy. Still, Bakar couldn't help but be impressed by these mountain men who had strong horses and powerful medicines, and who were obviously skilled fighters. Were these truly the same men whom Captain Harat routinely referred to as "savages" and "barbarians?" Bakar began to realize King Artavazd had been wise to exclude the Captain from this mission, after all.

"Friend, this is the way to your village?" began Bakar. "That is where we were headed before the ambush, but I am not sure we would ever have found it without your assistance."

The tribesman grunted, then nodded sharply.

"Your contingent was scaling the mountain that separates our land from that of the accursed Mardeni tribe. Had you gone on much further, it would not have been in our power to protect you."

The difference in the man's dialect was strong, and not one Bakar had ever heard before, but it was easy enough to understand.

"Well, as I have said, we are most grateful for your intercession," Bakar replied.

The tribesman grunted again and, with a simple gesture of his arm, said, "We have arrived."

Bakar looked up, but all he could see was a small clearing surrounded by mountain walls, rocks, and a few trees, a small frozen stream – there were no people, no houses. Nearby was a small waterfall, already frozen from the biting early winter, mostly concealed by a small cluster of trees. Bakar imagined in the summer when the trees were blanketed with foliage, the waterfall would be entirely invisible, perceptible only from the clamor its waters undoubtedly made as they crashed onto the rocks below.

Then, one by one, Tibareni villagers began to emerge from the edges of the clearing. Instinctively, the Royal Guardsmen, including Aro and Bakar, drew nearer to one another. Bakar turned in the direction of Vahan's hearty laugh and saw Tigran next to him, smiling.

"Welcome to our humble village!" Vahan called out.

Only then did Bakar realize their group had, in fact, arrived in a village, though an extraordinarily well-concealed – if primitive – one. The mountainous walls and the path hidden by trees offered an ideal camouflage from neighboring tribes.

"If our guests would kindly dismount and follow me," said Vahan with a gesture toward the waterfall. He and his tribesmen went first, but Bakar, Tigran, and the others stopped short when their hosts disappeared behind the columns of ice that made up the waterfall.

Tigran looked at Bakar hesitantly, but then shrugged his shoulders and said to his men, "Well, we have come this far..."

Leading the group, Tigran slipped behind the waterfall through a narrow opening in the rock. Bakar followed with the others close behind. To Bakar's astonishment, the small opening widened almost immediately into a surprisingly immense cavern lit from above where shards of rock had fallen from the roof of the cave and opened the interior to the outdoors. Inside, it was clear that the Tibareni village was much more than an unassuming clearing with the few rocks and trees observed outside. Here was the heart of the village; a safe zone for what looked like a hundred or so Highlanders.

The village was bustling with life. In one area, vines and beams had been used to fashion a wooden floor where villagers carried out various activities. In another area, several small rooms were sectioned off using the fallen boulders, or the addition of wood logs, for walls. In one area where a larger part of the ceiling had caved in, swine and sheep grazed under the open sky. Just beyond them were flint and arrow-makers busy at work. In the center was a large fire that took some of the chill out of the frigid Highland air. It was surrounded by tables, with pots for cooking suspended overhead.

When Tigran and all his friends were safely inside the inner village Vahan spoke.

"We are sorry for your losses, but you will be safe here. Our women will see to it that you have food, drink, and shelter."

A few Tibareni women were standing in the vicinity regarding the strangers with something between curiosity and suspicion, but when

Vahan nodded in their direction, they dispersed quickly to make them at home.

"My men will tend to your remaining horses; rest now, but I advise you to remain on this side of the waterfall during the night. We will speak more about your business here in the morning; I think we have all had enough fun for one day."

With that, Vahan turned and disappeared into one of the thatched shelters.

The village was crude, but its people were thriving with whatever the Highlands gave them. Bakar admired their loyalty to the lands they called home, unforgiving as it was. As he looked about with unconcealed astonishment, a young village woman approached him bearing water and a clean cloth. She caught Bakar's eye when she was just steps away.

The girl smiled shyly and gestured for Bakar to sit next to her by the fire. She looked down at the items in her hands.

"For your wounds," she said.

"Oh, but your tribesman tended to my wounds in the woods," replied Bakar, who could not help but be enchanted by the girl's demure glances. She was pretty; her face delicately framed with silky auburn hair and accented by dark, serious eyes that shimmered when she managed the courage to look at him.

Bakar sat so she could have a better look at his wound, which was now blistered and blackened from the mysterious salve. The pain he felt from the salve had dulled now almost to the point of numbness.

"You see," he said, "the medicine he used has stopped the bleeding."

The girl looked at the charred gash and laughed quietly, bashfully. Her voice lilted in Bakar's weary ears like soft music.

"That medicine," she said, drenching the cloth in the water then wringing it between her small hands, "will burn clean through your leg if it is left on too long. It was meant as a temporary measure, only to keep you from bleeding to death in the wilderness."

"Oh," replied Bakar, feeling his cheeks blush. He was the one avoiding her gaze now. "Then I guess it is good I met you."

# Chapter Eleven

Dawn rose on a calm morning. Vahan dressed and sat himself next to his dying fire. A cook arrived shortly thereafter, handing him a meal of steaming mash in a bronze bowl.

"Where did you get this bowl?" asked the Tibareni chieftain, turning the piece in his hands and admiring the gleam it cast in the morning's first light.

"It was a gift from our visitors," replied the cook, "along with many others such as bronze tools, more bowls, even some trinkets for the children. Just before dawn, the Prince himself gave me this assortment of rare spices. I can't remember the last time I cooked with these; they are nearly impossible to cultivate in our poor excuse for soil."

"Prince, huh?" Vahan replied with a shrug, and the cook left him alone.

Vahan could not eat without some measure of unease. It was true that the gods were not kind to the Tibareni during the last harvest. Their food storage was lower now than ever before, and winter was only just arriving. Spices like the ones Tigran brought were luxuries the Tibareni had learned to live without. What they needed was more options for food and weaponry, so that they could use their surplus of horses for trade, instead of feeding themselves in times of famine.

As he forced himself to eat, Vahan reflected on the difficult year his tribe had faced. If the food shortages weren't enough, the unrest certainly was. In addition to the usual trouble from the neighboring Mardeni tribe, Vahan had just recently battled to the death with a fellow tribesman who wished to overthrow his leadership and assume the title of Chieftain himself. The man was trying to stir around the idea of attacking the villages and towns to the south, but he didn't have many followers. His hopes were that if he took Vahan out, everyone else would follow him. In general, Vahan's leadership was well respected amongst the villagers, but as the upcoming winter dragged on and food was scarce, something like that was bound to happen again.

Vahan stepped out into the open cavern with the bowl still in his hands. He saw Prince Tigran emerge from his sleeping quarters and make his way toward him.

The Tibareni chieftain sighed. The Prince seemed a genuine enough young man, less entitled than others who made the journey before – but what did he *want*? Vahan was growing impatient with implications from the Capital that the Highlanders owed something to the Crown. Even if he felt the slightest inclination to capitulate to their demands – which he most certainly did not – this generation of Tibareni had nothing left to give.

"Good morning, Vahan," said the Prince as he approached.

"*Prince* Tigran," replied Vahan. "Have you eaten?"

"I have, I was awake just before dawn."

"Excellent," Vahan said, handing Tigran his now empty bronze bowl, "then let us go for a walk. I trust you have much to discuss with me, though I will admit I am not sure how much I have to say to you."

Vahan gazed at the puzzled Prince out of the corner of his eye as he looked at the bowl that was handed to him, then finally just put it down and followed him.

The men headed for the waterfall. Now that it was daytime, it would be somewhat safer to venture beyond their little village. On the other side of the waterfall, sunlight dotted through the trees in the clearing. The air was cold, always cold, but the day promised to be gentler.

"So, Prince Tigran, let's not waste each other's time with pleasantries," Vahan said. "Tell me why you have journeyed so far from home and risked your lives to see me. I am not sure whether to be flattered or deeply suspicious."

"King Artavazd sent me," replied Tigran simply. "I was sent to see if our men and yours could be allies. I admit many are not fond of many aspects of your way of life up here – but I believe the King has room for all of us."

Vahan laughed, but Tigran remained serious.

"You will forgive my hesitance in believing Artavazd wishes to be so innocuous," said Vahan. "I recall tales of a time many years ago when the people up here agreed to unite and create this Armenian kingdom of yours, for the sake of your old grandfather, I believe."

"You lost many men in those wars," remarked the Prince.

"Yes. My own great uncle was one of them," Vahan replied softly, then more angrily added, "and once it was all over, we were abandoned yet again in these harsh lands to fend for ourselves. We were given none of the kingdom's fertile lands, no security, no titles. Your 'great' noble families would have been too offended if any of their privileges were shared with us. The only things we received were requests for taxes and tribute – a fine thanks for the lives we sacrificed."

"I cannot deny that you were grievously wronged – and I cannot but commend you for the lives you have carved out for yourselves here in these most inhospitable lands. I daresay any of the nobles in our court would be dead before the first frost."

"I daresay they would," Vahan replied without concealing a scoff.

The two walked in silence for some distance while Vahan contemplated the King's possible motives. A long time had passed since the Crown "invited" the Highlanders into the fold – and to Vahan's knowledge it never occurred with so innocent a motive.

The Prince was a polite young man, who was either naïve and sincere, or cunning and deceitful. If the former, he must be a pawn in some scheme of the King's – but what? And if they were in fact after something, Vahan doubted that the Prince was foolish enough to think he could get it without a fight – a fight that he and his tiny contingent of men would have no hope of winning as long as they were here in the Highlands.

"My men and I are most grateful for your heroism on the plateau," said Tigran after several moments passed, "we are anxious to repay the favor and do what we can to strengthen the ties between ourselves and your tribe."

*Well, if this prince from the city means to be friends, let us see just how friendly he intends to get.*

He turned to Tigran and said, "In fact, there is a serious problem that the Tibareni are facing now, though I am not sure what *you* can do to help. At the heart of the issue is the Mardeni tribe. There is a controlling group of young men, an ignorant but vicious bunch – a most unfortunate combination. You have met some of these scoundrels already; they are the ones who attacked you and murdered your friends yesterday."

The Prince appeared thoughtful. It was obvious to Vahan he was struggling to control his anger at the way his guardsmen and their mounts had been ruthlessly slaughtered on the plateau yesterday by these same men.

"They are an ongoing source of trouble for you?"

"Constant in recent months," Vahan affirmed, "but their current chief is not the problem. He is in fact a very old man who has not desired conflict with us for many years now. The trouble stems from his nephew, Iratu. He is a weakling and a fool who harasses the most vulnerable to make himself feel more powerful."

"But why would he act so dishonorably?" asked Prince Tigran. "He must know that such conduct does not befit a chieftain."

"Iratu is power-hungry and jealous," explained Vahan, "and he is not the one who will be chief next. His uncle refuses to hand over his leadership to him, and Iratu is too much a coward to earn the title for himself by challenging the one chosen to claim the Mardeni title of chieftain to a death-duel. Instead, he recruited a group of wild young men from his tribe and they ambushed and killed many of their fellow tribesmen who were of any worth. They have since been terrorizing both our tribes with attack-and-retreat tactics, robbing the food we need to store for winter."

"I see," said the Prince, and it did seem as though he was closely following. "Why don't you join with the other Mardeni to oppose this vile group?"

"There has been too many attacks and retaliations now, and many in both tribes harbor hard feelings towards each other. Worse still, it seems some of the remaining men of their tribe are holding back from doing anything about it, preferring to see who will win out before picking a side. Eventually, I believe I can come to a friendly arrangement with their future chieftain, if there is anyone left from either of our tribes by then."

The Prince again seemed to take it all in, nodding to himself with his brows creased.

"Is this future chieftain of the Mardeni tribe a very powerful man?" he finally asked.

Vahan smiled. "No – *she* is a very powerful woman."

"A woman chieftain," exclaimed the Prince. "That is highly irregular. But this Iratu cannot defeat a woman?"

"On the contrary, Iratu terrorizes many women – and children too – whenever he sees fit. But *this* woman is the Mardeni chieftain's grandchild; Mari is her name, and she was raised as a son. I daresay her skills in combat rival any man's."

"Astonishing," said the Prince, still deep in thought. "And this Mari is an honorable person?"

"Honorable means different things to those in the Highlands," Vahan said. "But there is no question she would be the wiser choice."

"I am sure there is something I can do to help," Tigran replied. "How soon would you be willing to put a plan into action?"

Vahan couldn't help but be impressed by the Prince's apparent desire to be of assistance. "The sooner, the better," he said. "Our rivalry with the Mardeni tribe has become more than a mere inconvenience. It threatens to escalate into a full-fledged war."

"Let me think on it, I believe there may be a way to appease everyone. Well, almost everyone," Tigran said with a sly smile playing at the corners of his mouth.

Vahan's gut told him that Tigran's intentions were sincere, but he would still have to see what the Prince was planning.

"OK then," Vahan said with a smile. "For now, why don't you help me procure dinner for the tribe?"

The Prince smiled back and nodded. "Please lead the way."

When Bakar awoke, the afternoon sun was shining brightly through the many holes in the cavern's roof. Not quite believing it could be as late as it was, he dressed quickly and headed out of his sleeping quarters. All around him tribeswomen went about their daily routines. Most were too busy now to pay much attention to the stranger with the bandaged leg. Tigran and the others were nowhere to be seen.

Bakar walked slowly over to the tables around the large fire. He could bear a little weight on his wounded leg, but he was not confident it would carry him much further until he had some nourishment to sustain him. He sat down and moments later a bowl, of what looked to be legumes and grains mashed with a small amount of meat, was placed before him. Bakar nodded with gratitude, already beginning to eat.

Shortly before he finished his meal, he spied the girl who had dressed his wound the evening before. She was walking toward him with a shy smile; on her head and under her arms were baskets piled high with various hides. She placed all her baskets on the ground and sat next to him.

Bakar smiled warmly. "You are busy, I see."

"Yes," nodded the girl. She touched his bandaged leg tenderly. "I see your leg was not burned off, after all."

"Thanks to you," Bakar laughed gently. "You know, I can hardly believe how late I slept. I must have lost more blood than I thought."

"Your wound was deeper than it appeared."

"Again, I thank you – but how can I thank you properly when I do not know your name?"

The girl's cheeks colored slightly when she said, "I am Siran, sister of our Chieftain Vahan. And you are Bakar."

Bakar nodded. To him, she seemed as soft and skittish as a fawn, not at all like her gruff and commanding brother. He decided to change the subject before she fled out of fright.

"Have you seen the others? It seems I have slept through their departure."

"Prince Tigran and my brother went hunting earlier this morning; they have not yet returned. I believe your guardsmen went with them. And your archer friend –"

"Aro."

Siran nodded. "Aro spent much of the morning speaking with our arrow maker, then he volunteered to go off on patrol with some of our warriors."

"Ah, that is very like Aro," Bakar said, "and it is good that the Prince and Chief Vahan are getting better acquainted. He seems to be an honorable man."

Siran looked pleased. "Your Prince also seems honorable," she said. "The manner in which he arrived here reminds me very much of a poem of sorts that my grandmother used to tell me, which was said to have originated by an oracle in these very mountains."

Bakar's curiosity was aroused. "What do you mean?"

"*A reluctant Prince is for what I await,*" Siran recited, "*my words are for him and his possible fate. He will come to me after he is saved, he will leave from here when time to be brave. Decisions he will make that will reach near and far, our kingdom he will make rise tall, or fall hard.*"

"That is very interesting," Bakar said, then slowly repeated the poem out loud. Of course, there were many princes and many such poems and stories from seers, augurs, oracles and the like, especially regarding royal figures or famous warriors. But still, it was intriguing enough that they were presented with this poem here and now, on a journey with a prince who was urged into the undertaking by his uncle king.

"What else can you tell me of this oracle?" Bakar asked.

But Siran could not elaborate; "I am sorry, that is all I know about it, but perhaps my brother may be able to tell you more. Bakar, I have already sat too long. Perhaps we shall have another chance to talk before you and your men take your leave."

"I hope so," said Bakar tenderly as he watched her re-balance the heavy basket upon her head and secure the other two under her arms. She offered him a hint of a smile before turning and heading in the direction of the shelters furthest from the fire. Bakar longed to follow her, but did not wish to draw attention to himself by disrupting her daily duties any further.

All in all, Bakar could not deny that *these* Highlanders, at least, were exceedingly welcoming. Still, he could not forget all of Harat's reproaches and warnings against the tribes in these lands. Their dreadful battle the day before was proof that not all Highlanders were as friendly. He hoped the remaining members of the Royal Guard were doing their duty, and that the Prince was not in harm's way out there.

He needn't have worried. Within a few hours Bakar was sitting around the fire with Aro as well as Prince Tigran and Vahan, who had returned from their hunt with a modestly sized deer.

As their dinner turned on a spit over the flames, Bakar mentioned the brief story Siran told him of an oracle nearby, and recited back the poem for them.

Prince Tigran's face lit up with wonder, and he made Bakar repeat it yet again. Bakar did as he was asked, and when he was done the Prince quickly asked Vahan, "do you know anything more about this?"

Vahan nodded. "Yes, I have heard stories of this oracle, who is supposed to live in a cavern near our very mountain. Legend has it she came to these lands as a child among the entourage following the defeated General Hannibal of Carthage, when he came through this part of the world while on the run from the Romans. The stories go that when they were passing near this area, this special little girl felt the need to stay here, and has lived in this area as a hermit for these many, many years since. No one really knows how old she is, though if the stories are true, she has lived a life at least three generations long by now. These stories and poems surface through the years from those few who have actually sought her out and succeeded in finding her. I have never come across her myself, even though her supposed dwelling area is said to be only a half-day ride from our village."

"Well, I must admit that poem is intriguing," Tigran said. "And the legend that she came here with the Great General Hannibal maybe more so! It was my own grandfather who allowed Hannibal to take refuge in our kingdom, then he and Hannibal became good friends while he was here. It is said the famous general helped with finding the location of and planning our Capital city of Artashat during that time. I am now very curious to find out if this oracle exists. Vahan, do you think you could find her supposed dwelling place?"

"I wouldn't mind trying," Vahan replied with that now familiar smile of his. "It would be interesting to find out if you're this *reluctant prince* from the poem."

"Bakar, will you be well enough to travel tomorrow?" Tigran asked.

"I should expect so," replied Bakar, rubbing a hand over his wound. Already the swelling was diminishing and Bakar felt confident that another night's rest would make him strong enough to accompany Tigran. Bakar didn't think the Prince would be so taken by the story, but his enthusiasm to find out more now made Bakar just as curious and interested in this seer as the prince.

Their friend Aro was less enthusiastic. "I have seen much today of the Tibareni's skilled horsemanship. You would scarcely believe the stamina and strength of these small beasts; it seems we have done our own Caspians a disservice by breeding them larger. At any rate, some of the villagers have offered to teach me their ways of handling horses in this unwieldy terrain so that I can still shoot straight on horseback. I would very much prefer to stay behind."

"Very well," Tigran said. "Bakar and I will venture out tomorrow with two of our guardsmen. I will leave the others behind to accompany you."

"I will bring a few men as well. Do not fear, we should be safe enough," Vahan added, "This area is not near that troublesome Mardeni tribe that attacked us. I have never seen this old seer with my own eyes, but I daresay that poem has intrigued me now as much as it has you. First thing tomorrow, we'll head out to see what this ancient woman has to tell us."

Bakar realized quickly this was not an undertaking Captain Harat would approve of. *You will be taking extra risks in a dangerous area for no good reason,* was probably what he would say. He realized there was truth to that. He could try and talk Tigran out of it; after all, then Bakar would have more time to speak with Siran again. But the Prince and Vahan seemed to be starting a genuine connection and it was good that they were both enthusiastic to do this together.

In the end Bakar decided to leave it alone in the name of continuing peaceful diplomatic relations. He only hoped the other tribes out there would feel the same way.

# Chapter Twelve

If Tigran thought the woods that obscured the path to the Tibareni village were dense, these woods were denser still. The horses kept their heads down to shield their eyes from the crisscrossing tree limbs, their wide heads burrowing through snow-laden branches. The sun had been shining when they departed from the village at dawn, but if it were still shining now, there was no way to tell through the thick canopy overhead.

Tigran rode in front of Bakar and behind Vahan who seemed, incredibly, to know where he was going. None of the men were inclined toward conversation given what happened the last time they had ventured through the woods on unknown trails. As a result, the hours of their day's journey passed so far with few words between them, even when they stopped around midday for a meal of mainly root vegetables and a little ale.

For whatever reason, the poem and story of the oracle had intrigued Tigran greatly, and he was eager to find her, but as more time went by, he hoped his curiosity wouldn't end up getting anyone hurt.

A short while after their stop, the trees at last began to thin. Tigran had gotten quite disoriented traveling in shadow all day, encroached upon by trees, but now he could see that, in the west, the winter sun was already slanting downward. He hoped Vahan really did know where he was going.

Just when Tigran was ready to tell Vahan that perhaps they should give this up and return to the village, the chieftain stopped their procession to examine an immense boulder a short distance from the path.

"Hmm," he muttered, stroking at his chin. "The tales say she lives in this area near an opening, beside what is described as 'a rock that does not belong'..."

Tigran looked around the area. The boulder did seem out of place, as there were no other noticeably large rocks in the area that he could see.

Vahan drew his sword and hacked at a few of the more obtrusive tree branches to get a better look around either side of the boulder.

"Yes, here," he exclaimed from the far side.

Tigran craned his neck to see what Vahan had found. From his vantage point, all he could see was the boulder and a small mound of earth next to it, both of which were surrounded very unremarkably by snow and tree branches. But then a look of triumph crossed Vahan's face.

"Alright, men," he said, "we shall have to dismount. Our horses cannot follow us here."

Tigran, Bakar, and the guardsmen dismounted to see what Vahan was talking about. Sure enough, there was a significant hole on the opposite side of the mound beside the boulder.

"The woman lives beneath the earth?" Tigran asked, incredulous.

"So it is said," replied Vahan.

"Incredible," said Bakar.

"You stay here to watch over the horses. Be on your guard," Tigran said with a nod to one of his guardsmen.

Tigran saw Vahan give a nod to one of his own men, who turned to stay behind as well. With that, the rest of them crouched down to slip through the opening one-by-one. They went in the same order in which they were traveling, with Tigran in between Vahan and Bakar. As he crept through the hole it quickly became evident to Tigran that, much like the clearing in front of the waterfall entry to the Tibareni's village, this dwelling was much more than it appeared on the surface.

Shortly after passing through the hole, Tigran saw a ramp made of earth that led further below the surface and opened into a room of considerable size. To Tigran's surprise, there was a soft glow of light coming from the other side of the cavern, so it took little time for his eyes to adjust to the sight before him.

To his astonishment, the first beings he spied, and smelled, were not of the ancient female variety, but common goats and chickens which were bleating and clucking contentedly. The animals grazed and pecked their way through small patches of grass that grew on the ground near openings in the westernmost earthen wall where narrow streams of the setting sun punctured through. Tigran was amazed; it appeared that they were traveling along a mountainside under which the old seer's home was hollowed out, though as far as how and by whom, he couldn't imagine.

The warmth from the lamplight and cheer from the small spots of sun would have made the large room a most comfortable respite from the afternoon chill above ground, were it not for the filthiest of stenches also pervading the space. The fetid odor was enough to make Tigran wretch.

Bakar came up next to Tigran, his cape over his mouth and nose, and whispered, "There – in the corner. I think the foul stench comes from her."

Tigran followed Bakar's gaze. Indeed, in one corner lay an impossibly old woman. She sat in a heap, leaning against the wall behind her. Her hair was long and matted, like withered snakeskins that coiled from the crown of her head down into the tangle of crunchy dried reeds upon which she sat. She was filthy from head to toe and apparently blind. Although she gazed intently in the men's direction, her eyes were half closed and clouded over with a milky yellow film, thick enough to obscure the color of her irises.

Tigran was stunned by the sight of the crumpled old woman who seemed to be – before their very eyes – decomposing and crumbling into the earth that surrounded her. Was this the oracle of whom Siran and Vahan had spoken? Was she even alive? The putrid smell that emanated from her suggested otherwise.

"So, he has finally come."

Though barely audible, the croak of her voice startled them as if she had jumped out of hiding and shrieked. She struggled to lift one arm and gesture about the room. Sighing heavily, she said, "You men enjoy these beasts for a hearty meal after I am gone. This dwelling was first made by your ancestors after all, long before even the Athenian Xenophon and his band of mercenaries passed through these lands centuries ago."

Tigran looked at Bakar then at Vahan, who were both looking back at him as if thinking, as the Prince was, this day's journey would very likely turn out to be fruitless. An oracle conjured images in his mind of mystery and wisdom, potions and prophecies, like the stories of the mystics in Delphi at the Grecian Temple of Apollo. All they saw here was an ancient, foul-smelling woman in rags, whose dwelling was a dank tomb filled with nothing but hapless beasts. It made the Prince feel something like pity, certainly not awe or wonder.

Still, they had journeyed a long way and risked his men's lives yet again, all to meet this purported seer. Tigran decided to speak to her.

"The 'he' you mentioned...is it me you speak of?" he asked.

"Who else would it be, that smelly mountain man you are traveling with?" The old woman's feeble voice said, moving her blind stare to the Prince.

Tigran heard Vahan ask Bakar, "Is she talking about you?"

The rest of the men, still standing close to the entry, shifted uncomfortably.

"Why? Why would you be waiting for me?" Tigran asked of this strange old woman.

"*A reluctant Prince is for what I await,*" the woman recited back to them, "*my words are for him and his possible fate. He will come to me after he is saved, he will leave from here when time to be brave. Decisions he will make that will reach near and far, our kingdom he will make rise tall, or fall hard.*"

"That's the poem," Bakar said, surprise punctuating each word.

Then she said, "I see my message has reached you. Are you not the Prince who has come for his possible fate?"

"He is a Prince. And we did save him when he arrived here," Vahan answered before the Prince could.

Without moving her yellowed gaze, the old seer drew a slow breath in and began to speak.

"This land called to me when I was a child, before I even knew what the gods meant for me, or what I was. But I know now that I am one of the last of my kind, perhaps the very last. For a new age has befallen the world; an age where my gods of earth, air, fire and sea are worshiped no longer."

She smacked her lips together over toothless gums.

"Each of us has a destiny, sometimes big, sometimes small. My little destiny was given to me after I arrived here. It told me to stay and abide here, and convey to those who found me what my visions foretold of their lives. And during these very many years there have been some who did find me here...though I fear fewer still ever took heed of the words given them. But through those visitors I sent hints into the world of my other visions that they might find who they would...who they were meant to reach..."

"That's how we came to know of the poems and tales," Vahan whispered.

The ancient woman then drew another breath and lowered her head. When she didn't move for long moments Tigran leaned in a little closer, but then almost jumped back again when she suddenly raised her unseeing eyes in his direction and continued.

"You, young prince," she said, her words edged in relief, "*you* were the one those visions were for. And you will be the last...*you* have a big destiny. One far grander than you can imagine."

She nodded knowingly, her sightless eyes focused on some distant time only she could see.

"Now I know you are the one for whom I've been waiting. The one for whom my body yet lives and draws breath."

"But why, why me?" asked the Prince once more.

The old seer sighed again before answering.

"Perhaps to say that your destiny may lie with your own people and not with those whose glory and power you covet."

Tigran gasped, taking an unconscious step backward. The room was just as it had been, the stench, the chickens pecking about, the warmth and the damp – but in that moment something changed. Moments ago, he was all but convinced that this was perhaps the worst oracle the world had ever seen. Now he felt exposed, betrayed. How could she know his own doubts, his own longings? This had to be some kind of trick.

"The larger fates, the fates of kingdoms and empires, are wrapped in your own."

She bowed her head again and shut her eyes. She seemed to be concentrating; the words came slowly and were punctuated by uneven breaths and pauses that made them wonder if she might be sleeping.

"You, your people, these lands, or the power and ambitions of the other – in the end, you may only have one of the two destinies you seek: burn bright now and have what you will in a faraway land, before you fade away... Or return to your own, where your name may remain for many, many more years after today's qualms are long-gone memories."

Tigran stayed silent, but protested inwardly. *If it is Parthia and Armenia she speaks of, why can't I have a little of both? What could this ancient woman who has apparently been living underground for a lifetime really know about me anyway? This is all crazy.*

Then the old seer looked up from her lap with surprising haste and faced the Prince once again. Could she really see him through those diseased eyes? Tigran shuddered at her stare.

"This all may be crazy," she said then, and suddenly the hairs on the back of Tigran's neck rose, "and you *will* get both, though it will bring you much sorrow. And in the end, you will *still* have to choose. You will always have to choose."

"Tigran, can you make sense of what she speaks?" Vahan asked him.

Tigran did not answer him. He could hardly believe what he was witnessing. Was she really seeing his thoughts? Did she actually know of his possible fates? He stared back into those sunken milky eyes for a long moment. She nodded her head slightly, though her eyes were still looking past him.

He believed. He believed her, and it shook him to the core. He knew at that moment that he would never be able to have all that he wanted, that he desired. He would never be able to keep one foot in Parthia with the other in Armenia. He would always be forced to choose one over the other.

"Tell me more," Tigran finally said.

"I have told you all I had to," she replied, sounding relieved, "but I *will* tell you one more thing."

Tigran leaned in now to listen closely.

"You are young," she continued, "but you will not always be. One day,

if your years number as mine do now and you have chosen well thus far, even with all your continued triumphs and sorrows, you will be faced with yet another decision, still another choice to make. This final choice will truly test you, and put the future fate of your people in your hands yet again. Remember, your destiny informs the destinies of many. I am sorry you shall never have the luxury of idle foolishness that so many do."

"What is this decision I must make? I don't understand," Tigran pleaded.

"I can say no more," she said.

"Please," said the Prince, desperate now for answers he feared, yet nevertheless wanted to hear. "What is this decision?" Tigran knelt to one knee before her, not hiding the anguish he felt. "Please, you must help me, what choice should I make?"

The oracle simply shook her head. Then she looked up towards the ceiling of the cavern.

"Your greater destiny is only now beginning, but my little destiny has been fulfilled. I have accomplished all that I had to. The time for my kind is ending, and I am ready... Ready to return to my own ancestors now."

These last words spoken, she rested her head against her chest and closed her eyes. Tigran and the others waited some time for her to speak again, but when she did not, the Prince finally braved to lean in closer once again. Hesitantly and with great reluctance, he reached out to feel for a breath.

There was none. The old seer was dead.

---

Even though the Tibareni generally took the wisdom of oracles seriously, Vahan prided himself on being more reserved with his faith. Still, the event that had just taken place seemed ominous indeed. There were many apparent coincidences that led the Prince up to the point of meeting the oracle, a woman who seemingly had little purpose but to deliver her cryptic messages to the Prince and then breathe her last.

"Believe me, I am as dumbfounded as you are," said the Prince, who seemed to have taken notice of Vahan's furrowed brow.

They had spent the night outside the cavern, by the boulder, and departed at first light, animals in tow. The going was slow, and they found themselves walking their horses much of the way.

"Quite a series of events," nodded Vahan, but he could not resist adding, "Tell me, Prince Tigran, what do you make of the old seer's message? Why would she have to remind the King's nephew, the Prince of Armenia, that his destiny is in his homeland and not elsewhere?"

"I am sure I don't know, is that how you understood it?" replied the Prince, but Vahan thought he detected the faintest waver in his voice.

"A self-evident prophecy if ever I heard one," remarked Vahan as he eyed his companion warily from under raised eyebrows, "unless, of course, you *have* set your sights on a kingdom that is not your own."

Tigran averted his gaze and did not answer. Vahan was sure that his words struck the heart of the matter, but he decided not to press the Prince further.

Vahan was fairly confident the "others" the old seer had mentioned were not the Highlanders, since that would be a step in the wrong direction for the Prince, at least in terms of the "glory and power" he apparently sought. But if he did not seek greater control and influence in Armenia, then where? And what would become of Armenia if he chose a destiny elsewhere?

*Oh well, he is here now. Prince Tigran may have the destiny of Armenia in his hands, but for the present, he has promised his hands to a different matter entirely.*

For now, all Vahan could concern himself with was whether or not Tigran's bold plan to take out the wretched Iratu and his men would actually work. In the meantime – troubling message from the oracle or no – they were returning home with new sources of goat's milk and eggs, as well as a day or two worth of meat for his villagers. A meager success, Vahan conceded, but he was not in a position to turn his back on any good fortune that shepherded his tribe a few steps closer to spring.

"I hope this crazy plan of yours will work," Vahan finally said.

Tigran's expression adjusted quickly to the change of topic and he looked at Vahan with confidence when he replied.

"It will," the Prince said, "as long as we can convince Mari and her uncle, it will work."

"At least we will eat well tonight either way," Vahan replied with a smile.

# Chapter Thirteen

Roya woke and immediately began to pray. *Please, not again, not today.* After a few moments she sat up and took in a fresh breath of air. Then all of a sudden, there it was again!

Roya rolled over and heaved. Her stomach lurching, she tried in vain to make it to her relieving basin, but the vomit came out and spilled all over the ground and her sleeping gown.

"My lady," her younger servant girl said from the doorway, "Please, let me help."

Roya did not protest, and the girl knelt next to her and held back her hair as she finished emptying her insides into the bowl.

When she was finished, her servant quickly stepped away and brought back a wet cloth and began cleaning her mouth and hair.

"Please take off that gown, Miss," the girl said, "I shall clean and return it at once. No one shall know."

Roya gave pause to the girl's last comment, but forced herself to ignore it.

"I don't know what's wrong," Roya said finally, flipping her gown off her shoulders, "I feel fine later in the day."

The servant took the dress from the floor.

"Yes Miss; that is what I have heard happens."

This time Roya could not ignore the remark.

"What do you mean? It is an illness in my belly," Roya said dismissively "I probably just ate something bad; it will soon pass."

The servant girl looked up at her mistress, it was obvious she wanted to say more, but held her tongue.

"OK, out with it," Roya demanded in as friendly manner as she could muster. "What is it you want to say? I will not be angry with you."

The girl stood and leaned in close to Roya. Speaking very softly she said, "My lady, nearly three months have passed since...since your visit, you know, when your father was away?"

"Yes, yes," Roya said quickly.

"And as you know," the girl continued timidly, "I change and clean your bedclothes...you have not had your *other* visitor since then, you know..."

"Yes," Roya said, this time more slowly, her own logic and this girl's words both now forcing her to face what she did not want to think was true.

Roya was suddenly filled with panic. Even as she stood there in the nude, she felt her face and skin flush.

"Get me something to put on," Roya commanded, suddenly feeling extremely exposed.

If this young girl could tell her condition, her father would likely soon realize it himself. *If it is true,* she forced herself to think, *it doesn't mean...*

But deep inside Roya knew it was true, she was pregnant.

Her servant brought back a plain, dark dress and helped her put it on. Afterward, Roya stepped over to the bed and sat.

"What will I do?" Roya said out loud. Tears now filled her eyes.

"It is a blessed thing," the girl said carefully, "and your...friend, he will take care of you, I am sure of it. Do not be sad my Lady."

"Thank you," Roya replied genuinely, "but please, I must have your confidence, you must never hint of this to anyone."

"Of course not," the girl said, "but soon..."

"I know, I know. I will soon not be able to hide this."

The girl nodded, then went to retrieve Roya's soiled bedclothes and sweep the floor clean.

"Will you be needing anything else for now, Miss?" she asked, picking up the basin.

"No," Roya said, "I need some time alone...to think."

After the girl left, Roya laid back down on her bed, resting her hands gently on her belly.

*Perhaps she is right. Perhaps this is a blessing. Maybe this will lead to the Prince actually taking me as his wife much earlier than he would have otherwise. Or maybe he will be angry when he learns of this, as father surely will be. Maybe he will renounce me at the news.*

No, her Prince would take care of her, as the girl said, and as Roya knew in her heart. Their love for one another was true, and this could only bring them closer together. She had to believe that. In that moment she decided to write the Prince and tell him the news. She would plead with him to come back to her as quickly as he could.

Eventually she knew she would have to tell her father as well, but she would wait until there was no recourse, for he would surely be displeased.

*No, even if Tigran returns in time, I must have these weeks to shore up my courage and plan for the future, for who knows what direction father might go with this news.*

——•——••——•——

Ambassador Artaban was preparing for his meeting with the King of Kings. He was reading over the reports he had received during the last week from his people inside Armenia and the Royal Residence itself. In using his own informants, he could not only confirm other news he received, but would also get imminent information quicker.

Only today he received news that King Artavazd's health was declining still, thoughts were that he would not make it through the winter. It was very interesting news indeed, and something the King would appreciate finding out before even his own spies could inform him.

Artaban was also informed of young Prince Tigran going on an expedition of diplomacy up north, to the barbaric Highland territories. It was curious that his father would allow him go on such a dangerous mission, even though it was obviously ordered by King Artavazd. Artaban decided it was not something the King of Kings needed to know right now.

A rap on the outside of the open door to his reading room made the

Ambassador look up. It was the courier, another man on his payroll. Artaban almost forgot this was the day the courier would be leaving to make his way back to Armenia with small packages and messages and letters to and from the wealthiest and most important people. If there was anything being sent or received by anyone the Ambassador was interested in, the courier would let him know. It didn't hurt that the courier was also a master at forging seals.

"Have anything for me this month?" Artaban asked.

"Unfortunately, not very much," the courier replied in that raspy voice of his, "only one letter going out from that trader and his daughter that you told me to look out for. It is a letter the daughter is sending, going to the Royal Residence, for the young Prince Tigran."

"Well, that one may be interesting," Artaban said, standing and walking around his desk towards the door, "Have you read it yet?"

"No, I am running very late actually, was supposed to leave this morning, I was hoping you didn't care for this one."

For this man to presume anything made Artaban want to laugh; the simpleton, but then, that was why the man spent most of his time on the back of a horse.

"So, it has a seal then?" But Artaban realized from the man's tone it was so.

The courier sighed, "Yes, but they are using a new one now, and we haven't made a mold of this seal yet. It will take a few hours, hours I do not have right now."

Artaban was getting frustrated now for he, too, had to leave shortly, for his meeting with the King.

"Give me the letter and go then," Artaban said, irritation edging his voice, "messages get lost all the time, this can be one of them."

The courier held out his hand with the rolled-up scroll containing the letter. But when Artaban reached out to get it, he pulled it back quickly.

The Ambassador looked at him squarely, and then the courier held out his other hand, his empty palm pointing upwards.

*Not so ignorant when it comes to payment I see.*

He reached to his belt for his coin pouch, weighted it in his fist for a moment, then tossed it into the air. The courier caught it on the way down, smiled, and then brought forth his other hand with the letter.

"Always a pleasure," the man then said, dropping the scroll into his hand and turning to leave. "See you when I get back."

The Ambassador only grunted and turned back to his desk, breaking the seal on the scroll and unrolling the letter on the flat surface. He brought the lamp closer to hold down the top of the letter, holding the bottom with his own hand, Artaban quickly began to read.

*My love,*

*I am anxiously awaiting your promised return to Ecbatana this summer... not only because you are my love, but also because I have news. I am sure I am with child. Of course, it is your child, the result of our love. I must warn you, my father will likely be enraged when I tell him, but I will convince him that you promise to return and that we were already planning our lives together. I can only hope that will set his mind at ease. I expect the baby to be born before spring is through; it is my hope that this letter finds its way into your hands quickly, that you might come back to me as soon as possible, perhaps even sooner than planned... but I know you will come as quickly as you can, because I know that you love me as I love you.*

*I eagerly await your return so that I may once again feel the tenderness of your embrace,*

*Your Roya*

Artaban could not help but be surprised; this was not an event he envisioned he would have to deal with yet. He would have to think on this for a time, to see how he could most effectively use this information. He decided to leave this new finding out of his current report to the King. He rolled the letter back up, walked to his chest and laid out one of his travel cloaks, putting the scroll in one of the pockets.

*You will be safe there for now until I decide what to do with you.*

# Chapter Fourteen

Tigran stood on the ledge of an outcropping and gazed down along the valley below. "The sun will be going down soon. Do you think they will come?"

Vahan walked over to stand next to him. "I believe the old Mardeni chieftain trusts me. He respects that I have not yet called an all-out attack on his tribe for his nephew's transgressions. He promised he would at least hear what we had to say."

At this point, Tigran wasn't as confident as his new friend, and began to worry now if his plan would be done before it had even begun. He and Vahan had left the village alone and before the sun rose, in order to stealthily get half way around the mountain to the appointed meeting place. They had come early in order to make sure they were not walking into an ambush, then waited until the sun reached its zenith. But now, the sun was already beginning its decent, and there was still no sign of anyone approaching.

"I don't know, if anyone was arriving, we would be able to see them by now," Tigran said.

"Unless we didn't," he heard Vahan say from behind.

Tigran turned to see Vahan facing a woman. She somehow must have snuck behind them, but Tigran realized it was quite possible she had been around here the entire time.

The woman stood almost as tall as Vahan, she had light-brown hair that was braided tightly on each side of her head. She was wielding a short sword in her hand, with two matching daggers belted at her hips.

Tigran imagined the layers of clothing she wore afforded her some form of protection from the cold as well as combat. With wide, narrowed eyes, she expressed an accusatory expression, and her stance told them she was ready for anything.

"You are Mari, I presume," Tigran said gently.

"I don't know you," she said. "But from your accent and from what I can see, you are not from here. You," she poked her sword toward Vahan, "You I have seen and heard more of you, chieftain of the Tibareni. My grandfather promises that I can trust you."

"He did not come?" Vahan asked.

"He is too old to be sneaking around, and it is too dangerous for us both to be away from the tribe," Mari replied. "I convinced him to stay in hiding until I returned. He has left it to me to listen and decide on what you have to say."

"He must trust you very much," Tigran said, taking a step closer. "You can put down your sword, we mean you no harm."

"I'll be the judge of that, stranger," she said, not moving. "Now, tell me what you have to say. I take great risk being away from my grandfather this long."

"It's true," Tigran began, "I am a stranger to these parts. But I have come here to change that. As I've told Chief Vahan, I have come to learn about, and help to bring together, *all* the people of our kingdom."

Mari snickered, her brows raising over her big, round eyes. "And who are you to take on such a lofty goal?"

"I believe it is time to properly introduce you," Vahan said with mirth in his tone. "Lady Mari, may I present Prince Tigran of the Royal ruling house of Armenia."

"A prince!" Mari replied, this time with an outright laugh. "How lucky of me. I never dreamed to ever be courted by a prince."

"I don't think we're quite there yet," Tigran mused back. Then more seriously, he said, "Vahan has told me of the troubles with your cousin, Iratu. I dare say I have witnessed his work firsthand."

"Iratu and his men attacked Tigran on his way to find my tribe," Vahan explained. "Several of the Prince's men were killed."

"I apologize for my cousin's actions, he is a gutless coward who attracts the worst of men. Iratu strives for and feeds off of disunity, conflict and people's fears. He has put a wedge in our tribe which I fear will be the end of us all. If not for the few remaining tribesmen still loyal to my grandfather, he would already have taken over the tribe. As it stands now, he would have to challenge me for the title of future chief, but alas, he is fearful he will lose, which he certainly would, so instead he avoids me at all costs."

The care and passion Mari showed for her grandfather and her tribe showed Tigran she should be an honorable enough person; and her entire demeanor told Tigran she would be a formidable opponent for anyone.

"So, I gather you have no problem with fighting him, if he were to accept your challenge?" Tigran asked.

"I would love nothing better," Mari answered quickly and with conviction. "But as I told you, he is a coward, he only fights when he and his minions are at an advantage."

"Then let's give him one," Tigran began. "If you and your uncle can put your trust in Vahan and I," he then took another step closer and, reaching out for the tip of her sword, moved the end to hover over his own heart. "As I am putting my trust in you now; then I believe we can take care of your problem, and perhaps help bring your two tribes closer at the same time."

Mari gently pulled her sword back, then to Tigran's surprise, sheathed it. Her expression lightened, and she suddenly let out a deep laugh, as hearty as any man's.

"OK, *Prince* Tigran, you have impressed me and, if nothing else, you have courage. If Chief Vahan can put his trust in you, then I can do no less. Now, tell me this grand plan of yours."

———•━••━•—

Artos was readying his horse when he noticed Devo walking towards him. Though a few years younger than him, Devo had been his friend since childhood. But while Artos was from one of the strongest noble houses in the kingdom, the family that ruled over this Province, Devo was only a commoner, and thus, his station in life would always be limited.

"Hello, my Lord," Devo called out.

"Devo," Artos said in return, "how are things, my friend?"

"Good. Though I was beginning to worry when I didn't hear from you for three straight days."

"Yes," Artos acknowledged, "I was looking for someone. But I also had much to think on; I am working on my future. But I appreciate the concern."

Devo replied silently with a short bow. Artos knew Devo was completely loyal to him and that he would probably do anything he asked of him, but he never involved his friend in the more nefarious actions he was involved in. He never really gave much thought to why, but he was aware deep down that the reason was most likely for his own conscious, rather than for the good of his friend.

"Sire, your father seems to be in a particular mood today," Devo said then, "I heard him screaming something about taxes as I was rounding the main house."

Artos patted his horse's neck. "My father and brother are beyond frustrated that our old King Artavazd still breathes. They thought they would already be in the capital by now, my father as King's Adviser, and my older brother as Captain of the new Royal Guard. But it is not yet to be, and they grow more furious with each day that passes."

Though all that he said was true, Devo left out the fact that his father, in particular, was currently angry about missing funds, funds that Artos himself had *appropriated*.

Artos grabbed the reins and pulled his horse roughly to a walk. He tried desperately to hold back his anger and jealousy. But it was clear his friend was reading him correctly; Devo walked up next to him.

"My Lord, if I may; you cannot help the timing of your birth, but I have witnessed your greatness, I know of your intelligence, your tenacity. When your father and brother finally do go to the capital, you will effectively be in charge of our whole Province. And you will then be able show your father and the Kingdom your greatness, as well."

Artos felt his heart swell with pride, but if only others felt of him the way Devo did. No, his words were well meant, but he was wrong;

his father and brother would always be ahead of him, above him. Their greatness would always outshine his own. No, the only way he could truly rise to the top was to *remove* all those above him.

But to his friend, Artos only said, "You are a good friend Devo, not only my First, but my true friend as well. And I appreciate your words."

Devo didn't look satisfied, but said nothing else.

"Come now," Artos finally said as they arrived at the road, "Let's get the rest of my men together, we need to go out on another collection run."

"They won't be happy going out again so soon, especially when we still owe their payments for the previous time," Devo pointed out.

"Ah, but they *will* happily come along," Artos replied with a sly smile, "when I let them know I will be paying them in full for all past and present jobs."

That said, Artos tapped the two full sacks that hung tightly on the flanks of his horse.

"Just another hint at your greatness," Devo winked.

As their horses trotted down the road, Artos again thought back on that week at the Capital three years back, and that last day he had spent at the Guard barracks for their evaluation.

The first two days of the week were spent running, lifting and stretching, remedial tasks that Artos had found rather boring. By the third day they were still only practicing their footwork while wielding wooden swords, being watched all the while by that old Captain or his protege, the younger prince Tigran. By this point, Artos was not only beginning to get impatient, but also realized he was already far more skilled than the other initiates around him.

On that fateful fifth and last day, after a long morning of listening to the Captain drone on about safety, teamwork and other topics that almost put Artos to sleep, they were finally allowed to spar against each other. Though they were still forced to use the wooden, practice swords, by then Artos was eager for some real action and a chance to prove himself.

The boy chosen as his opponent was about his own age, but slightly larger. Artos faced him confidently, for he had already noticed earlier in the day his combatant held his sword too low when he tried to parry.

Artos had immediately advanced on his adversary, swinging his wood sword in a tight fore arc, followed by a back swing and then a quick trust to the mid-section that connected. The boy had stumbled backward, then fell down to one knee. He had dropped his sword and was grabbing at his chest.

Artos knew the air was knocked out of his foe, and he took the two steps closer to finish him off before he could regain his breath.

He remembered thinking; *even easier than I thought.*

He had raised his fake sword high, gripping the pummel with both hands and, with all his force begun to bring it down on his kneeling enemy...

"Ah, look there, a few of our men waiting for us now," Devo said, yanking Artos back from his memories.

"Good," Artos said. "I promise you, my friend, there will come a time soon when going on these runs will be beneath us both, and we will get what is due us."

"I have no doubt in you, my lord," Devo replied.

# Chapter Fifteen

Iratu's chest puffed as he watched with glee a long line of Tibareni armed riders riding off north at a gallop through the valley pass far below their lookout.

"There they go!" exclaimed one of Iratu's eight young disciples.

"Right on schedule!" said another.

"Quiet, fools!" hissed Iratu. "Our voices will carry far here."

They were perched on any icy ridge, hiding behind a thicket that easily concealed them from the riders below, especially at such a distance. They had set forth on this mission yesterday morning – and already he felt sure his cunning was about to be swiftly rewarded.

Iratu could not help but grin. He knew exactly where the Tibareni tribesmen were going, and why. Two days ago, their arrogant leader dared to send two messengers to the Mardeni village for an audience with his uncle, the tribal leader, and Mari, his bitch granddaughter. They sought permission to pass through Mardeni territory on a special hunt north of their border, one on which every one of their tribesmen would be going. They offered goats and chickens as gifts for the Mardeni not attacking their homes while they were away. His fool relatives had taken on the temporary peace-pact, and Iratu was sure they would keep their word.

Iratu had found this all out from his contacts still inside the tribe on the day it happened, and was preparing for it since. And now, far below where he was standing, off they went. Right on schedule. Every last one of them.

What really incensed Iratu was not that the Tibareni messengers hadn't been assassinated on the spot – though they should have been for their insolence – or even that they had been granted permission to trespass. No, what was most infuriating was that his old crow of an uncle had dared to include his cousin Mari in the meeting. The Mardeni tribe was rightfully his, not his whore cousin's. The idea of taking orders from a woman made Iratu's blood boil like nothing ever before, except for when he learned that he himself was not even a contender to succeed his uncle's leadership.

But now the tides were about to turn. The fool Vahan mandated that his village be emptied of its warriors in favor of a woefully ill-timed hunt. *They must be desperate to risk a hunt at this time of year when game is so scarce, and to take everyone at once...Now is my chance to show my uncle that those who underestimate me do so at their own peril.*

"They have all past," whispered one of Iratu's followers. "Do we follow?"

"No," said Iratu. "We head to their village."

The ride to the Tibareni village was uneventful, just as Iratu predicted. Had any of their patrols been left behind to guard the village, they would have run into them by now. The group stopped for a moment in the clearing outside the waterfall, which was also devoid of villagers. Behind the waterfall, Iratu already knew, was the entrance to the inner village. Though he had never been inside, he had spied one of the Tibareni tribesmen coming and going many times over the last months. *So much for the safety of a village hidden behind a waterfall. The safety is provided for its conqueror, who will come in, take what he pleases, and claim the land for the Mardeni – without a soul in the outside world the wiser.*

To his young men he whispered, "We will dismount here to make a quicker escape when we are through. Upon entering the village, kill anyone that remains, take what you want, and destroy the rest. The women you may do with what you like, but be quick about it – you will have as much of them as you desire when we have decimated the Tibareni Tribe once and for all."

Obediently, the boys dismounted, swords drawn, and followed their leader through the opening behind the waterfall. Iratu's heart pounded with exhilaration; he would claim the Tibareni land for his own and prove to his uncle he was a natural-born leader. *And then,* he grinned to himself, *I will make sure Mari gets the message, as well.*

But what awaited them in the inner village was not at all what they expected. Tables and chairs were knocked over. Linens, utensils, and trinkets were strewn about. Dishes were half-filled with food and the fire had been freshly stoked – but the village was abandoned.

"Someone has beaten us here," remarked one of the group, clearly disappointed. He sheathed his sword and moaned, "Now what do we do?"

"Quiet!" Iratu commanded. In fact, the village was not entirely abandoned; his eyes followed a trail of empty cups of ale, some discarded garments, and then two figures a short distance away. One of them appeared to be a drunken old man. He was lying face down in a cart of linens waiting to be washed. He looked unconscious, a jug of ale dangling from one hand. Beside the man was a thin figure in a hooded cloak who was trying to take a swig from the jug.

"You there!" Iratu called to her in a forceful tone, standing up straight. "What has happened here? Where are your fellow villagers?"

The hooded one also looked to be inebriated, and made no reply, but giggled softly and tried again in vain to drink from the jug of ale at the end of her companion's arm. Iratu and all his men approached, but stopped short when the drunken man stirred.

"What is it to you?" slurred the old man as he struggled to right himself. One by one, he peeled the soiled linens from his arms, his head, his face. Iratu tapped his foot impatiently, until a strange recollection began percolating within him; something about this man was definitely familiar.

"Uncle?!" exclaimed an alarmed Iratu. "What is the meaning – "

"Oh, nephew," replied the Mardeni chieftain, with no small measure of bitter amusement in his voice, "have you also come to visit the Tibareni?"

"What madness is this?" screeched Iratu. He was confused now more than ever, but the answers no longer mattered. Somehow he had been deceived – and if his pride was wounded before, it was nothing compared to his mortification now. It was time to show his uncle just how serious he was about claiming his rightful title as Mardeni chieftain.

He began to close in on his uncle, sword raised, but before he could take the final steps, an arrow swished by his left ear and pierced the ground a hair from his foot. Iratu looked up in surprise to see an onslaught of dozens more arrows hurtling down through gaping holes in the roof above. Moments later, four of the eight boys were dead on the ground, their still heaving chests perforated with arrows, the volume of their screams raising and lowering until they finally faded away.

The remaining four of his men dropped their weapons and scrambled for cover.

Of all the men in his group, only Iratu remained where he was.

His uncle looked at him very seriously, a most maddening air of superiority in his countenance. Then, before Iratu could raise his sword again, he was surrounded by twenty or so Tibareni tribesmen who must have entered the inner village during all the commotion. Closest to him was his enemy, the chieftain Vahan – and alongside him an obvious foreigner.

"Well, men, I'd say it was fortunate that we called off our hunt and doubled back to the village!" cried Vahan with a jeer. All around him, the most infuriating sound of Tibareni laughter filled his ears. "But Iratu," he continued, "your uncle tells me you would be chieftain – but you lack the courage to fight a *woman* for the title?"

Louder, more raucous laughter ensued until Iratu thought his chest would explode with ire.

"The bitch who thinks she's a man? I would bend her over and show her what it means to be chieftain!" Iratu bellowed. "Then, uncle, I would have your head on a stake as my walking stick!"

"Would you, now?" The mirthful voice – a mightily familiar one – came from the hooded one who had been perched by Iratu's uncle while he was disguised. Now, as the hood was lowered before him, Iratu realized with increasing anger that it was none other than Mari, the chieftain's self-important whore of a granddaughter. She was on her feet now, a short sword in her hand.

"Well, there she is!" Vahan taunted. "How fortunate. Now you can claim the title of chieftain sooner than expected! If you challenge her now, your uncle has sworn to me to relinquish his title to the victor. Take what is yours, Iratu, with my men and yours – wherever they are – as witnesses to your triumph."

The men around Iratu, still laughing and jeering and urging him on, now began to take paces backward to leave space for the duel. Iratu's eyes narrowed and his heart pounded. He could almost taste her blood, feel its warmth coursing over his hands. He looked at his uncle, who nodded his agreement, then to Mari, who wore her unrelenting, rage-provoking sneer. Iratu's hatred for his cousin, for his uncle, for all that was his due being stolen from him each and every day, was more than he could bear.

"I challenge you, cousin!" Iratu hollered.

With a frenzied wrath he leapt toward his cousin in a deathblow – but Mari ducked and slipped quickly over to his weaker side. He adjusted just in time for the swing of her sword to only graze his arm.

Iratu laughed madly as he rounded back with his own swing. Mari was ready for it; she ducked again and, in one motion, leapt at him while slicing the wrist on his strong side.

Iratu continued to laugh fiendishly, his eyes darting from Mari, to the jeering crowd, to his uncle and finally, to the outpouring of blood from his wrist falling onto his sword, which now lay at his feet. His laugh turned more into a high-pitched shriek as he raised his eyes to his cousin, who smiled as though the battle were over more quickly than she could have ever imagined. Then she raised her small, girlish sword, and plunged it into his throat.

———•••••———

By the following morning, Tigran, Aro, and the others were nearly ready to take their leave. They spent the rest of the previous day getting to know the Mardeni and putting the Tibareni village back together. But the worst of winter was approaching now, and if they didn't leave soon, they would be forced to spend months here before the paths were clear enough that they could make their way back home again.

The old Mardeni chief and his granddaughter, Mari, remained overnight in the Tibareni's village, along with some of their own soldiers – including Iratu's remaining disciples, all of whom were adequately humbled by the prior day's events.

Tigran took the invitation for them to stay, as well as its acceptance, as gestures of goodwill and gratitude on the part of both tribes. He couldn't help but feel somewhat proud – not to mention relieved – that his plan had worked out so well. Not only had he helped to stop an impending war, but he managed to befriend not one chieftain, but two. It was an accomplishment he was sure would impress his uncle – and perhaps even Parthia would take notice.

"Well, Prince Tigran, I daresay your idea of getting them together for the duel worked," said Aro, who had just reentered the inner village through the waterfall. "I will admit, I wasn't sure it was a good idea to send you and Vahan off into the lion's den without accompaniment, but things went just as you anticipated."

The Prince smiled. "I am pleased that the Mardeni chieftain and his granddaughter, Mari, trusted us enough to cooperate."

"Or hated Iratu enough to cooperate," interjected Aro with a laugh. "Either way, he was a thorn that all here are glad to have removed! And we got some measure of vengeance for our lost brothers."

"Agreed," said the Prince, peering up at the morning sky through the openings in the roof above. They had to depart now to get the best advantage of light and warmth from the daytime sun. "Are the horses ready?"

"I have just cinched up the last of them. The horses are waiting impatiently in the outer village."

Aro looked especially gleeful this morning, undoubtedly because his new friends had gifted him with a pair of pure mountain horses – one male and one female – for him to take back to Artashat.

Tigran looked about himself. Something – or rather, someone – was missing.

"Aro," he said, "have you seen Bakar today?"

Aro shrugged his shoulders. "I haven't seen him all morning, but I suspect he's with that pretty girl he met on our arrival here."

"A girl?" replied Tigran, not hiding his surprise, "I hadn't noticed – "

But just then, Tigran glimpsed Bakar and a slight young woman emerging out from under the waterfall. He couldn't be sure, but from this distance, it looked as though the pair were sharing a tearful goodbye. The girl put a hand on Bakar's shoulder and offered him a small peck on the cheek, then she turned and disappeared back behind the waterfall. Bakar stood for a moment in stillness before turning to approach his friends.

Tigran wanted to question his friend about the exchange, but Vahan was approaching with Mari, the new Mardeni chieftain, at his side.

That familiar broad smile crossed Vahan's face. It reminded the Prince of the first time they met, on the plateau in the mountains. That day seemed almost a lifetime ago. Prince Tigran returned the smile and extended his hand. Vahan shook his hand, and Mari followed in kind

"I thank you again, Prince; you are always welcome in the Mardeni tribe," Mari said.

"I must say I'm exceedingly impressed by how you are all faring here in these mountains. Our city dwellers could certainly learn a thing or two from your ingenuity and fortitude. I am sorry it is time for us to return to Artashat, but I am glad we are parting as friends. I only hope we can continue these friendly relations with our mountain brothers."

"Just remember, Prince Tigran," said Vahan, ever grinning, "friends do not ever have to *pay* for friendship."

The Prince nodded his head in understanding, looking both to Vahan and to Mari.

"Yours is a different world, that much is clear. I will make sure my uncle never asks anything of you but peace."

"Then let us keep the communications open, and I hope we shall see each other again soon," Vahan replied with a nod, his smile fading slightly. "But if you show up back here again with more than your handful of men, I can't promise your welcome will be as warm."

Tigran nodded with a smile of his own.

"I will be traveling to Parthia in the Spring, but we should be able to make another trip up here before that," he said.

"Ah," was Vahan's reply, "so, Parthia is it?"

Tigran's smile involuntarily vanished and he turned away, saying over his shoulder, "We shall meet again Chieftain Vahan."

"I do hope so, Prince Tigran."

# Chapter Sixteen

Winter had come and gone, but the coldness that penetrated the Royal Palace still lingered. The elder Tigran was perched at his brother's bedside. King Artavazd had been unconscious for nearly two weeks now. Tigran spent many of these last days right where he was now, with little more to do than stare at the trees outside the King's bedchamber window, which were just beginning to bud. If he loved his brother more, he would feel something akin to sadness and grief; as it was, his feelings more closely resembled impatience and frustration.

In the first days of this latest turn for the worse, the healers were in and out of the royal bedchamber with a steady stream of potions, elixirs, salves, and poultices. Now their visits were less frequent. Tigran was told that the healers did not expect the King to regain consciousness and that he was likely to pass at any moment. Two weeks later, the brother's dutiful vigil droned onward with no end in sight.

It is just like you to be so headstrong and unyielding. Tigran shook his head in anger. You breathe yet, but as usual, your breath serves no purpose but to spite me.

Still, Tigran had to concede that his brother's life did, in fact, continue to serve one purpose. As long as King Artavazd was alive, the elder Tigran would not be King. It was a responsibility he never wanted, but, then again, Artavazd used his kingship to make every conceivable bad decision, especially where Parthia was concerned. In the name of freedom, Artavazd stubbornly resisted a kingdom that would not tolerate resistance. If the King did not die soon, the price for that freedom would be the total decimation of Armenia.

Tigran sighed bitterly and rested his weary head in his hands.

Oh, brother, if you only knew of the many times I have intervened with the Parthian empire on our meager kingdom's behalf. Perhaps I did not save us with soldiers, as you would have wanted, but there is something to be said for diplomacy through resources. If our lands have prospered at all these twenty years, it is thanks to me and not you! But there is no glory in a bloodless battle, is there?

Somewhere beyond the distance of his thoughts, Tigran could vaguely hear a faint knocking at the door, but his memories won priority as he recalled one of the many times in his life his intellect was overlooked in favor of brute force.

It was many, many years ago, when the King was but a boy and Tigran younger still. He and all of his brothers were standing at the foot of their warrior father, the battle-hardened General and war hero who had succeeded in uniting Armenia and had begun a new Royal bloodline of kings. Despite the fact that his health was failing and his body creaked and moaned in pain with each demonstration, King Artashes was still trying to teach the boys the finer art of the short sword.

Neither Artavazd the eldest brother, nor Tigran showed any promise as warriors. On the other hand, the other brothers had a natural aptitude for fighting that they simply had not inherited.

How ironic that their fate was to die in battle for their weakling brother.

Although Tigran and Artavazd were nothing like their brothers as children, they also were nothing like one another. Artavazd followed their father's lessons with a most ardent determination, to make him proud despite a lack of talent. For his part, Tigran could scarcely bear his older brother's incessant pandering to their father. He had always known, even at that tender age, that swordsmanship would never be his strength. In the final moments of this memory, Tigran recalled his father seizing his wrist and trying to force the weapon into his small hand; he ran screaming from the field, and none of his brothers, and especially not his father, came after him.

The tapping at the door continued incessantly and was now increasing in its intensity. Tigran lifted his head from his hands with a heavy sigh to see Theo, the eunuch and head Royal House attendant patiently waiting for him to come out of his reverie. Theo kept a constant vigil over his king, doing everything he could to keep the King clean and comfortable.

Tigran finally motioned for Theo to answer the door. It wasn't opened more than a few inches before Ambassador Artaban pressed his way into the room.

"Sire, I left Ecbatana as soon as I got word, but the swollen spring rivers slowed our progress. The King... Is he..?"

"Ha!" scoffed Tigran, rising to his feet. "You, here to pay homage to your ailing monarch? I can't remember the last time you were actually in your mother country."

Artaban looked to be on the verge of protesting, but Tigran raised his hands in a gesture of peace and took a deep breath to calm himself. Although he and Artaban had always gotten along, it was mainly because the bulk of their interactions were via letters and messengers. Truth be told, Tigran didn't trust Artaban any more than his brother did; it was perhaps the one thing they did have in common.

"He breathes still," said Tigran, sitting back down, "but that is about all. We try to force food and water into him a few times a day, but he takes in very little."

"A travesty," replied Artaban, casting a cursory glance in the direction of Theo. When he looked back at the elder Tigran he said, "Do you mind if we speak alone?"

Tigran grunted, then nodded to Theo, "I believe it's time for you to do rounds of the palace servants to ensure they are not taking this opportunity to procrastinate in their work."

"As you wish, sire," the eunuch said, but he didn't look happy about leaving his King's side.

When the door closed behind him, the Ambassador came to sit next to Tigran.

"This is a crucial time," Artaban told him, "I come bearing news from Parthia. The great Mithridates, King of Kings, comes to visit our fair Armenian capital. He wants to personally ensure that the impending transition will be... smooth. He wants to meet the new Armenian King."

Tigran's mind raced. Transition? Smooth? The King of Kings coming here...would he bring his army, most likely he would...

He thought about his son, who was eagerly awaiting the spring thaws for another visit to Ecbatana; the Prince would not want to miss the opportunity to welcome the King of Kings here in Artashat. But young Tigran was not here. His brother had agreed on his son's plan to bring an absurd amount of supplies to his new "friends" that they could not otherwise acquire without his assistance. The young Prince had pressed Artavazd about it the whole winter through, but Artavazd had not given him an answer...at least until he realized the Prince meant to take another trip to the Parthian capital in early spring. King Artavazd had assured both Tigrans there would be time enough for the journey to Ecbatana upon his return from the Highlands, but the elder Tigran saw his brother's ill intentions as clear as day.

The fool would have done anything to keep my son from Parthia, Tigran mused, recalling how his brother had fallen unconscious just a day after the Prince's departure back north.

But if Mithridates was on his way, then the houses loyal to him would be pleased, and those houses that were not, well, they might have good reason to be worried...where is this line of thinking leading me?

"Yes," he replied distantly to the Ambassador, his gaze elsewhere, "perhaps King Mithridates' presence would... help."

Artaban nodded, "Sire, if I may be so bold, everyone knows King Artavazd is all but passed. I heard news of it as soon as I crossed the border between our lands. Your people are already in mourning. The crown is all but yours."

Tigran's faraway gaze persisted; that accursed crown was the last thing that would tempt him now. Everything would now be on his shoulders. Tigran simply sighed and said nothing.

"Still," Artaban pressed on, "there are a few houses loyal to your brother who are using this most unfortunate situation to cause unrest wherever possible, more every day. It is essential that we secure the leadership of Armenia once again so we can put an end to any notions of upheaval and end this civil unrest."

He paused, but again Tigran didn't have a reply for him, so he resumed in a lower tone.

"Would it not be better for the King of Kings to see upon his arrival, that your succession has already taken place? Perhaps it would be best if we did not – how shall I put this? – delay the process any further."

Tigran's faculties came back to him in full force upon hearing these words.

"Ambassador! What are you saying?"

"Only this, Sire: I can see you are very tired and in dire need of rest. Your country needs you now; you must take care not to fall ill yourself," said Artaban, his voice dripping with the most tender of concern. "My own healer made the journey with us from Parthia. Let him watch over King Artavazd while you get some much-needed rest. By the look of it, it is very likely he will pass during the night, I am sure. I will personally maintain a constant vigil, and be sure to come and get you after... well, if anything happens."

At first, Tigran did not know how to reply. It was true that his brother was all but gone now. Delaying his own assumption of the crown was only postponing the inevitable and could very likely make the transition all the more problematic. He supposed there was little harm in expediting the process now; in fact, the sooner Artavazd was laid to rest, the sooner the insufferable mourning vigils and visits of condolence would finish... and the sooner he and his son could attempt to put the shards of their alliance with Parthia back together.

"Yes, I admit I am very tired," Tigran replied slowly. "I will take my leave now for a rest, but do let me know as soon as – if there is any change."

The Elder Tigran took a last, side-long look at his sleeping older brother before he stood and quietly left the room.

———•—••—•—

When King Artavazd opened his eyes, he felt as if he were floating on his back in a calm, warm-water sea. He breathed in deep, and was surprised when the painful coughing fit did not follow. When Artavazd looked around, he realized he actually was hovering in the air. Under him, he could see what looked to be the top of his younger brother's head, along with that of Ambassador Artaban. They were hovering over someone laying in rest.

A moment later, Artavazd realized who that person was.

So, the time has finally come.

Suddenly there was a flash above him, and he looked up to see a huge swirling circle of bright, white light. It called to him, urged him to come through.

He knew what it meant, he'd been fighting it for years now.

He looked down again and saw his brother stand, head bowed and back bent, and leave the room.

He watched as Artaban then bent over his body.

Have it your way then; I leave it to you... I am ready.

He reached up towards the light, and it drew him in, until the light was all there was.

Artavazd opened his eyes again and, immediately felt himself to be in a state of complete peace and happiness. He felt no pain; he looked down and brought a hand to his chest, only to see and feel the strong, hard body of a man in his prime. He sat up and stared in wonder at his arms, torso and legs. He brought his hands to his face, and felt smooth, unwrinkled skin. It was his own body, only as it was when he was a much younger man.

He looked around and saw that this time he was sitting on soft, green grass, near a meadow with colorful birds flying about the lush trees. The air was fresh and warm, and small, puffy white clouds floated in an otherwise stark blue sky.

He stood, then heard laughter and pleasant music coming from beyond a nearby bush. He began to walk towards the sounds, and could soon smell freshly fired meats and the scents of spices and strong wine.

His mouth watered and he found he was smiling as he passed the brush to see what awaited.

He walked into a courtyard, with two grand palaces flanking the flat, grassy square where a crowd of people were gathered.

As he neared, Artavazd realized about a dozen people were sitting around a large table, chatting, eating and laughing, as a few young women in white robes played happy music on lyres with shining strings.

A woman stood and turned to look at him. He squinted to recognize the beautiful young lady, with long brown hair and sparkling green eyes... Those sparkling green eyes... Nazani?

His wife recognized him as well, and ran to him, her arms spread open. The next moment, Artavazd was once again embracing the only love of his life, the woman he had lost all those years ago. He hugged her with all his might, promising himself that he would never again let her go. They held each other's faces, both streaming happy tears now, and exchanged smiling, watery kisses.

After a few moments, still holding her hands, he backed off and looked her up and down. She was just as he remembered her, before...

"All is well now, my love," Nazani said with that wide, inviting smile of hers.

"How, where," Artavazd stuttered, some small part of him still trying to make sense of all that was happening.

"No need to worry about that any longer, my love," she said, half turning and waving back towards the table. "Look, everyone is here, and they will be so pleased to see you."

A young man stood up, tall, built and handsome. He had thick brown hair, green eyes and a strong chin. He walked over to them, his expression seemed as puzzled as Artavazd's own must have.

"This is Zoravar," His wife said gently.

The name meant 'powerful', and it was the name they had chosen for their infant boy, before... How could this be, their baby had died only weeks after he was born...

"Zoravar, this is your father."

Artavazd could feel that it was true. They embraced, and his son was strong, a man among men.

"Come, join us," Nazani said, waving again towards the welcoming table of others. "We have saved a seat at the head of the table for you."

Artavazd nodded to his son, who smiled back and returned to his seat. He then walked to stand behind the chair set for him and, looking upon the guests, he saw all of his long-lost brothers. They were telling stories and drinking merrily with their wives and children surrounding them. He also saw his daughter-in-law, young Prince Tigran's mother, still as beautiful as she ever was... Still healthy. She smiled at him and mouthed, 'thank-you'.

At the other end of the table was his father, looking just as young and strong as he himself was now. He lifted a giant mug of ale in solute to Artavazd, nodding slowly with a proud smile on his face. Then his father took a long swallow and went back to his hearty debate with the giant of a man sitting next to him; another proud looking man with his hair pulled back in a single knot behind his head and wearing a silver-studded leather vest with a shape of an elephant carved on the chest. Hannibal the Great.

Artavazd knew this was where he wanted to be, where he belonged now, and he wanted nothing more but to embrace it. But, the kingdom, the Parthians, did he not still have much to do?

"Sit and relax now, my love," Nazani's gentle voice gently urged. "You have no reason to worry any longer."

He sat, and his wife reached over to put her hand on top on his. "My love, your part is done. You have accomplished all that was needed of you. Most of all, you know in your heart, the kingdom's fate will be in your nephew's hands now."

Of course, she was right.

And so, finally, Artavazd embraced his peace.

# Chapter Seventeen

The winter had slogged by at an excruciatingly slow rate, but now the snows were finally melting and the way North was clear once again. Tigran felt bad for leaving while his uncle looked to be in his worst state yet; many said he would not make it through the winter, but his tenacious uncle proved them wrong. But now, what little remained of his health seemed to be melting away with the season's snows. The Prince continued to remind himself that he was preforming his uncle's last wishes. He just wished the King would be around to see it accomplished.

Tigran and his friends were now leading a small caravan laden with supplies and food. This was the second time he led his own expedition, and he was intent on not losing any more people this time.

The first few days of their travels were relatively peaceful. But Tigran had relented and brought Babandur with them this time, so only a certain level of calm could be had. Tigran knew very soon they should see the town of Tasha over the horizon, the last northern town before venturing into the mountainous Highland territory.

Tigran was riding at the head of their procession when he heard a horse trotting up closer from behind.

"Tigran."

It was Babandur, his giant friend. He should have been able to tell from the hard footfalls of the horse. Babandur came up alongside him and, indeed, when Tigran gazed at the other horse's face, he got the impression the steed was thinking, *why me?*

"I know," the Prince said before Babandur could continue, "you are going to ask me how much longer now, am I correct?"

"No, that's not what I was going to ask," Babandur replied in a mocking tone, "I was going to ask if there are any ladies of worth at this town we are heading to. I dare say the towns so far have been fielding nothing but disappointments."

"My friend," Tigran said, "this is a diplomatic mission, as I told you before we left, we are not here for our enjoyment."

"Bah," his friend scoffed, "what is life without enjoyment!"

Another two horses rode up to his flanks and Tigran knew without looking that it was the rest of his friends he'd brought along on this second voyage; Bakar and Aro. Merak stayed behind, and Tigran was thankful that it was his friend's decision and not his own. Merak's body did not respond well to riding a horse for long periods of time, and he would have slowed them down greatly.

"If any of you are going to ask how much longer until we reach Tasha, the Prince does not want to hear it," Babandur said when they were all within earshot.

Tigran couldn't help but smile.

Aro was the one to answer. "You big oaf, we all know we're almost there, we made this journey just before winter."

"Ah yes, I remember now," Babandur said in an exaggerated manner, "another time you left me behind. Remind me again why?"

"You are beginning to remind me why," Tigran said sternly, "now, do not make me sorry I brought you along this time."

Their colossal friend's shoulders squared up a bit and, as his back stiffened, his head looked to rise even higher into the air, but he remained quiet.

Then Bakar exclaimed, "There it is, I can see the top of the Inn."

Tigran saw it too, and if they both saw it, obviously their bird-eyed archer friend Aro had, as well.

"I never asked how you were able set this meeting up in town," Aro said, "I'm amazed the Highlanders would venture down this far."

"I must admit, I was surprised as well," Tigran said. "We were able to exchange several letters through the winter using my uncle's contacts in the northern Provinces. Chief Vahan was actually the one who suggested he and his men could meet us here in order to help escort our goods for the last, and most dangerous, part of the journey. It turns out the Tibareni tribe had contact with this particular town of Tasha before, mainly because of the proximity to their own lands. In the past, they traded pelts and mineral rocks for food during especially hard winters."

"I liked the people we met here both times we stopped on the last trip," Bakar remarked.

"Yes, they have gained a reputation for being a most tolerable people," Tigran agreed, "evident in the way they welcomed us the first time we were here, and that they are willing to trade with the Highlanders."

"Yes, but how are the women?" Babandur said to himself, but loud enough for all of them to hear.

"It is only a very small town, my friend," Aro replied, "I'm afraid the pickings will be slim."

"Remember," Tigran pointed out, "I don't want any foolery while we are here. These are a humble, peaceful people, and I do not want to make them regret hosting us."

Just then riders could be seen approaching from the direction of town. Tigran could not help but take in the dramatic scenery before him; the four horses galloping through a flat stretch of grassland with the huge, snow-capped mountain range hunkering down behind them

"It's your friend Vahan," Aro said, squinting with a cupped hand above his eyes, "along with a few of his men."

A few moments later Tigran held up a hand to greet their new, would-be allies.

"Hello again, Chief Vahan. As I promised, we have returned."

"I see," the mountain man responded, flaunting that usual smile of his, "and you have brought the supplies you pledged as well."

"Yes I have," Tigran responded, "but you may not like the use I would have for most of it."

Vahan's brows creased, but when he saw the Prince smiling back at him, his tension seemed to ease.

"Well, Prince," he replied, "if this new scheme of yours is anything like your previous one, I am very curious to hear it."

"I'll explain it to you, my friend," Tigran said, "but let us talk over a nice meal, and a comfortable couch wouldn't hurt either."

The tribal chieftain let out a loud laugh and eagerly turned his worse around.

—•——•——

Harat looked about the forum, eyes squinting through the early morning sun. With winter's retreat, the city center hummed with activity, increasing a little more each day as longer, warmer days were ushered in. In every direction were vendors setting up their wares for a promising day of trade. Fruit and spice carts lined the perimeter of the forum where passersby would most likely be drawn in by their rich fragrances. Nearby were cloth and clothing carts, as well as vendors selling handmade toys, clay cooking utensils, and copper and silver jewelry that glittered in the sunshine. In the very center of the forum were several wine and ale vendors, where weary shoppers could rest, enjoy some refreshment, and perhaps purchase a few drops for their evening meal.

The Captain wove his way between the many carts, each tended by men and women who shouted over one another to get his attention. But Harat was looking for one cart in particular and, when he found it, he reached for the small pouch of coins fastened to his belt. Upon hearing the jingle of the coins, the old merchant instinctively looked up from his work.

Dressed as a Parthian, the man was busy pulling packs of silk and fine linens off his mule to be showcased on his small cart. He was ancient, much older than Harat, with shriveled skin like burnt bacon, the result of a lifetime of travels from market to market.

Harat untied the pouch from his belt and tossed it to him. With the reflexes of a much younger man, the old merchant moved in time to catch it. He fingered the leather of the bag without opening it, then harrumphed loudly.

"The last of my children has died. Ye gods, even some of their grandchildren have died, having already lived a full enough life. And I, well, I shall die very soon myself, out on the dusty road, and my mule will probably have a feast of my corpse."

Harat raised an eyebrow. "And?"

"*And*," scoffed the merchant, clearly impatient, "I don't need your money any longer. Your debt has been paid a thousand times over. How long has it been now?"

"Over fifty years," said Harat.

"Fifty years since those bandits stopped you – just a stupid young boy then – you and your friend outside the city."

Harat could not help but feel mildly wounded by the remark, but he steeled his exterior and refused the pouch of coins when the old merchant offered it back to him.

"They murdered my companion and I was next," Harat said. "You saved my life; that debt cannot ever be fully repaid."

"Oh, nonsense," the man replied, tossing the pouch on his cart and waving his arms in dismissal. "You were a terrified child; those thieves had no honor. It was only my intention to remove two dishonorable men from this world that you might have a chance to become the honorable Captain Harat."

"I fear the world has not fared much better for it," said Harat, still squinting in the sun. "Our kingdom is in peril now at the hands of a man with far less honor than those two pitiful thieves."

He lifted a sleeve to his brow to wipe the beads of sweat forming.

The old merchant turned back to his mule to unpack and assemble his weight scale. After setting it down, he retrieved several iron balls and balanced them on one side of the scale, then the other. Satisfied it was calibrated correctly, he spoke.

"King Artavazd was an honorable man indeed. I was dismayed to hear of his passing."

"Yes, well, it is a loss that I fear spells trouble for Armenia," replied Harat, "even though the King lived perhaps longer than he should have. In these last years, he was kind and well intentioned, but frail. The unification of Armenia achieved by his father has slowly been worn away by outside influences and unmitigated greed."

"And his very own brother," the older man added.

"Yes," Harat agreed, "Armenia has been torn apart from within and, in the years where it really counted, our King Artavazd was quite unable to do anything to stop it."

The Captain sighed as he surveyed the withered old man's cart, which was now stacked high with fine cloth, sure to command a healthy profit on such a cloudless day. The King was dead and his heathen brother now sat on the throne, but Artashat's citizens still had mouths to feed and children to clothe and houses to tend to. Life did not stop. Even though it was dealt a foreboding blow, it trudged onward, as ever.

About to take his leave and let his old friend get on with his business, Harat made a small bow of respect. Upon rising he found the merchant staring at him intently as if trying to come to a decision. Then he cast a quick glance over each shoulder and stepped closer to Harat.

"Over these many long years you have refused my help; refused to hear what I could tell you of your Parthian enemy."

"I would not make a spy of you," said Harat. "I despise spies."

The old merchant held his gaze. "Listen to me boy. This was the last journey for me through those accursed mountains; I will never know why we sing the praises of that thin, punishing mountain air! After today, I take my wares south and I shall not stop going until I reach warm ocean shores, or I breathe my last."

It was a threat the Captain had heard many times before. Still, every year this ancient cloth merchant who had become as a father to Harat returned to the spring market on the anniversary of the day he had saved Harat's life, and every year Harat paid him a visit.

Because he made his home in Parthia and traveled through so many cities between, the merchant knew much of the happenings thereabouts, but Harat never asked him for such knowledge. To do so would have been a breach of honor Harat would not dare make, especially to a man who had risked everything for his sake. But something about the old merchant's demeanor was different this time, more urgent. Harat sensed this may, indeed, be the last time he would lay eyes on the man who had given him life.

"Go on, then," said the Captain in a low tone. "Tell me your news. This one time."

"The King of Kings deigns to visit the Capital," replied the merchant, "he is coming now."

"Ecbatana?" asked Harat, though the sinking feeling in his stomach told him otherwise.

"Artashat," corrected the merchant, his eyes serious. "King Mithridates comes to *your* capital in Armenia. He has assembled an army; I passed them not one week ago while I was traveling here, then made haste through shorter routes where an army of such a cumbersome size could never pass. Nevertheless, by now they cannot be more than a week or a little longer away."

Harat was silenced for a moment by this most unsettling news, then began to fume. *It certainly did not take long for Ambassador Artaban and our pathetic new king to lay waste to Artavazd's legacy.* The King of King's army marching through Armenia would boost the confidence of those nobles that were for Parthia, while most likely helping to eliminate those Houses against them. Harat realized that any Province opposed to their new King's policies was in grave danger, especially if they were anywhere near the path of the King of King's approaching army.

Finally, with as much composure as the Captain could muster, he said, "Perhaps it *is* time for you to move your wares south."

The old man looked at Harat with a mixture of concern and resignation.

"And perhaps you could accompany me this time?"

Harat shook his head. "You know that is impossible, *especially* now."

"I feared so," nodded the merchant.

They locked eyes quickly for one last time, then, without ceremony or words of farewell, he returned to his wares, arranging the silks and other cloths so they would attract the eyes of eager shoppers. Harat stood in place for only a moment before turning and marching back in the direction of the Palace, this time with a purpose more steeled, and a conviction more sure than ever before in his long life.

# Chapter Eighteen

It was late in the day when Artos returned to the house, and the estate glowed under the red and orange skyline. He noticed three horses out front, walking about untethered. *What is it this time?* As he neared the house, Artos heard shouting from inside. But the noise did not convey anger. No, instead it sounded like joy and happiness, and this made Artos all the more curious.

He dismounted his own steed and, leaving him untethered as well, quickly ran up to the partially open front door of the house.

"...Yes, it is true! Tigran is the new king. We leave the day after tomorrow. My son, our day has finally come!"

His mind worked quickly and Artos realized what had happened. The King was finally dead, and the day his father and older brother had desperately been waiting for had come. The blood in his veins pulsed now with a new ferocity, for Artos knew that *his* day had come as well. The day when he must decide, once and for all, if he would do what was needed for the chance to rise to his true greatness.

Artos walked inside, airing an expression of innocent curiosity. His mother was by the backroom doorway holding his newborn sister. His younger brother was standing next to her. It looked like mother had been getting his siblings ready for bed.

By the main dining room, his father and brother had taken seats at the head of the table. A servant arrived with two mugs of wine for them.

"Bah," his father exclaimed, "this will not do. We must truly celebrate tonight, for after tonight, more important work begins for us, and we will have to restrain ourselves from there on. So bring us a few amphora!"

They both laughed and embraced in their shared joy. Artos fought hard to try and match their enthusiasm.

"Father, brother," Artos said from the doorway, "you are correct, you deserve to celebrate as never you will again. I will get the jars myself." Then to the servant he said, "you can go now, I will take the honor of serving my father and brother for the rest of the evening."

"Ah, my son Artos," his father suddenly called, waving and spilling his wine towards him, "I know you are not happy that you will not be following us to the capital, but know that I have put my trust in you to watch over the Province, during the times your brother and I are away from the estate."

Artos' jaw tightened for an instant, but he doubted either of them noticed. He finally said, "I am honored by your faith in me, father. I will go get the wine."

He rushed through the back of the house, but made a quick stop in his room to get something he needed first. Artos then went out back to the dry-house where, half buried in the ground, was the giant earthenware vessel which held their storage of wine. He pushed over the heavy, flat rock that sealed the vessel, and moved over two empty amphora.

Before he filled the wine, he reached into his tunic and pulled out the small folded cloth he had taken from his room. He carefully unfolded it and stared down at the reddish-brown powder within. His heart was racing and he felt beads of sweat forming on his forehead.

Artos forced himself to once again bring forth the memory of that last accursed day at the Royal Guard barracks; the day that forced him to realize the path he must take to reach his own destiny. In his mind's eye, he was transported back into his body from three years ago.

He had just taken down the boy they put up as his opponent in the sparring bout and, with his wooden sword raised over his head in both hands, was about to drop his final strike down on his foe...

...In the next instant, it felt as though he struck a boulder; his arms thundered in pain and his sword fell from his grip. Artos jumped back, his first thought was if his still-tingling arms were broken. He saw that his wood sword had broken in half, and the pummel had fallen from his numbed hand.

He looked up to see Prince Tigran standing to the side, the flat of his real, metal sword still held out over the head of his kneeing opponent.

"Yield," the Prince said. "This is only a practice session, we are not here to intentionally hurt each other."

"I only fight to win," Artos replied, his veins bulging in anger. His arms were not broken and the numbness was subsiding, but the strike to his pride would never abate.

The Prince lowered his sword, but didn't sheathed it. "I have noticed during this week that you are already very skilled," Tigran said. "I know you may be getting impatient, but Captain Harat is not only looking for initiates skilled in combat, he rather favors a person's character and discipline above all. Do you understand?"

Artos straightened his back and glanced around to see all other sparing had ceased, and the other boys were all watching them with dropped jaws. He was sure that a naiver person might think the prince was trying to help him, but Artos could almost feel the condescending air of superiority underneath the Prince's comments, and it made his blood boil.

Artos moved his eyes back to the Prince, envisioning himself bludgeoning his head into the ground.

"I understand," Artos said through gritting teeth. "This is all a waste of my time, there is nothing for me to learn here."

"It's a shame you think that way, friend," the prince said. "But trust me, there is much more to learn here than the swordplay."

Artos knew when he was being patronized. *He thinks he's so much better than me because his uncle happens to be king.*

"If you pardon me saying, *oh prince*," Artos said. "I think your Captain, hero and great warrior though he once was, is now past his time. He'd be better off teaching little children how to walk."

Artos wanted to wipe that smug, confident look off the Prince's face, and it seemed the comment about his mentor hit the mark.

Prince Tigran's face turned red and his jawline tightened. Artos was sure he could take the prince down, but he couldn't be the one to strike first this time. Whether he won or not, the Prince could always have him executed or sent to the dungeons if he so chose; It was nothing less than Artos would do in his position.

"Watch how you speak of the Captain," Tigran said.

"As you command...*Prince*," Artos replied. "I have no choice but to obey your highness' wishes, as I'm sure the Captain does as well. That is the reason *you* are here, is it not? Entertaining yourself as second to the Captain, with your real sword, watching over us while we play like children with wooden toys."

The Prince sheathed his sword, and then, to Artos' surprise, unbuckled his belt, letting it and his sword, drop to the ground.

"If you think I carry favor here because I am a prince, you are more a fool than you are letting on," Tigran said.

"Forgive me," Artos replied. "I would like to show you just how right I am, but again, you *are* a prince, and could have me beheaded at your whim. For that reason, I am sure nobody has had the courage to show you how little you actually know."

"And you think you have the courage," the prince asked. His hands were balled into fists now and his own eyes filled with rage.

"I do," Artos said calmly. "Though I also like my head just where it is."

Prince Tigran snickered. "Fear not! As everyone here will be our witness, there will be no repercussions for your actions from this moment on," he said, stepping forward with each word. "Come then, you brazen fool, show me how little I have learned."

"As you command," Artos said, lurching forward suddenly, then down for a leg sweep under the approaching Prince.

The Prince jumped over his leg, then as they both straightened once again, he tried a kick of his own, which Artos easily dodged.

They circled each other, fists raised, feinting in and out, until the prince finally came in with a right fist which just grazed Artos' jaw. But he realized too late it was only another feint, and a second punch from the princes' left fist struck him in the side of the face.

Artos could feel the blood rushing to his cheek, and he was sure he heard laughter from the other boys over the ringing in his ear.

He bent over, sucking in his breath and holding out a hand over his head. He was looking down when he saw the Prince's feet fall into his shadow.

"Are you hurt," the prince was still saying when Artos suddenly lunged at his midsection. The prince fell on his back, and Artos leveled himself on top of him.

"You see," Artos said, dropping a fist across the prince's face. "I *am* better than you." Another punch drew blood out of the prince's nose. "And I am only the second son of a southern lord."

Artos raised his fist again, centering all his anger into a final strike, when the prince twisted his hip and managed to free himself enough to unexpectedly ram his forehead up into Artos' face.

His ears rang again and the ground weaved under him through tearing eyes. He lashed out again, fist after fist, but nothing landed.

He was pushed over and the Prince forced his way out from under him. Artos quickly struggled to get back on his feet, even as he still fought to gain his focus.

Another blow slammed him on the side of his face, dropping him back down to his knees. Artos looked up, his legs failing him now, to see the Prince's bloody face hovering over him.

"Do you yield now?" Tigran said.

"You think your so much better than me," Artos grunted. He brought a hand to his lip, which was thumping in pain, and wiped away a strip of blood.

"What is the meaning of this?" Hollered the deep voice of Captain Harat from behind them.

"Artos, what are you doing?" the next voice put more of a shock into Artos, for it was his own father's.

Artos turned to see his father, his older brother, and the Captain standing there, flanked by the equally shocked spectator initiates.

"We are invited here by the royal family themselves, and you are fortunate enough to try out for the Royal Guard, and *this* is how you decide to conduct yourself? The Prince, by all rights, could have you killed right now!" It was the angriest Artos had ever seen is father reach.

"I told him there would be no backlash for this, and I agreed to the fight myself," the Prince said, wiping blood from his face.

"That is of no matter," Captain Harat replied. "You have disappointed me today, my prince, but we will speak of that later. I have watched this boy all week now." Harat turned to his father then; "My decision is already made. I am sorry, my Lord, but I do not think *this* son of yours is right for the guard."

"I understand completely, Captain," his father sighed. "And, Prince Tigran, please accept my humble apologies for my insolent son, he will not ever bother you again. Artos, come now!"

Artos raised himself and kept his eyes down as he walked past the Prince and the others. He had never been so embarrassed or made such a fool of himself, and it was a day he would never forget.

*You should not have made a promise you couldn't keep, father...*

Artos was back in the present once again. The open cloth with the red-brown powder inside still lay in his upheld palm, but his hand was now shaking. His heart was pounding so hard he thought it would burst from his chest, and free-falling sweat was stinging his eyes.

*I have to do this, this is the moment I've been waiting and planning for.*

A short time later Artos returned with the two amphora of wine, and happily filled and re-filled his father and brother's cups, as they continued to drink and laugh merrily while they forecasted their shared futures.

It was sometime later when Artos burst into the back room of the house. His mother, younger brother and infant sister had long gone to sleep, and they awoke with a start, their eyes adjusting to the small lamp held in Artos' hand.

"Mother, brother," the tone in Artos' voice confirmed their alarm, "you must leave the house immediately, a fire has broken out in the dining room!"

"A fire?" his mother said in panic, "your father and brother!"

"I will get them out, but you must gather the children and leave now!" Artos commanded, a different kind of panic in his own voice.

His mother obeyed, even as smoke began to enter the room. She grabbed the baby and pulled his younger brother to her side, and they all ran for the front door. Artos followed them to the doorway, then waved them to go on.

Artos ran back inside, but then slowed himself to a measured walk as he made his way to the dining room doorway. The room was now completely engulfed in flame. Tongues of fire began to lick and take hold of the very walls surrounding him now, but Artos stayed as long as he could, gazing on the still bodies of his father and brother. They did not scream, or even move, as the blaze overwhelmed their bodies. Artos was sure they wouldn't, for he had put enough poison in the wine to take out four horses.

Finally, as part of the roof began to cave in, Artos turned and, covering his mouth with his hand, rushed through the smoke and outside. He turned back to see a couple of servants free themselves from the burning house as well, one of them partially on fire. Then he went to his mother and brother huddled on the ground; they were in shock, and crying now. Suddenly there was a loud crash and Artos saw that the entire house was now a complete blaze of fire, carrying black smoke high into the early morning sky.

"I'm sorry mother," Artos said, looking down at his mother and siblings with pity, "I could not reach them, the flames had already taken them. I believe the fire started there, but they were too drunk to realize what was happening around them."

His mother, her face smeared in dirt and tears, only looked up at him plainly, expressionless. He panicked.

*Does she know? No, she could only suspect, but she will never know for sure.*

"We are fortunate I woke when I did, and at least had enough time to save you and the children," Artos said, looking her back sternly.

Their past was burning before their very eyes and their new future awaited. By the time the sun rose Artos would truly begin his rise to greatness as the sole ruler of his House and the Province.

*I should have taken things into my own hands from the beginning.*

He realized now it was a mistake trying to pay someone to take out those in his way. He already added the man he paid for the failed effort on the Prince to his list of victims to exact vengeance on; after all, two new spaces had just opened up. Artos had searched for that contractor of assassins himself to no avail, but he was sure he would find him sooner or later.

The order of his intended victims had changed, and he would have to be patient for his next opportunity to take out the younger Tigran, and that old Captain as well. He was more confident now that he would be able to eliminate all those who stood in is way, all those who deserved his vengeance. The Capital, the Guard barracks, the new King's ear... soon there will be nobody left in his way, and Artos would have all of it in his grasp.

# Chapter Nineteen

Only a day after meeting his old friend, Harat and a dozen veteran Royal Guardsmen, found themselves lined up across the entire width of the Palace throne room. With them was also young Merak, looking ill at ease in a row of larger, stronger, braver men. He had opted not to go to the Highlands with the others because of the long ride and almost assured danger; but now, standing here in the throne room, it seemed as though Merak had something to fear at home, as well.

Opposite the Royal Guard and its Captain was a new throne, made entirely of stone and commissioned especially for the new King Tigran, First of His Name. It was rumored that the King of Parthia himself had gifted the throne, which sat empty now. Merak leaned in to Harat.

"What are we doing here?" he whispered. "Why has the entire Guard been summoned to the King?"

"Shh!" was the Captain's only reply, but the truth was Harat had similar questions – questions for which he feared he already knew the answers. Yesterday, when Harat had demanded an explanation for King Mithridates entering Artashat with such a considerable army, the elder Tigran insisted this was no raid or threat; the King of Kings was merely paying a visit to the new King of Armenia, and of course he had to bring his warriors for protection. But Harat knew the Prince's father to be a coward, and now, when he was most vulnerable, it was no surprise that his cowardice reared its head in the most destructive way imaginable.

*And what a show the Parthian army will make to any who would oppose our new king*, thought Harat with a bitter shake of his head.

At last, the great main doors into the throne room creaked open just enough for four of King Tigran's attendants to come filing out. Behind them came Ambassador Artaban, then the King and, finally, four large, menacing-looking men – strangers – armed and armored with the finest equipment Harat had ever seen. Each of these men held ominous banners: one of an eagle with a sheep in its claws, one bearing a wolf, another with a horned goat head, and one bearing a vertical spear flanked by two stars. Harat recognized them instantly as banners from four different noble houses from the far south and east regions of Armenia nearest the Parthian borders and the Royal Road. They were among the few Houses who supported their new king unconditionally.

Merak fidgeted anxiously.

"Please, Captain Harat," he whispered again, "what is happening here? Why do these mean looking men seem to be protecting the King? Shouldn't the Royal Guard be doing so?"

"Quiet!" Harat replied sternly, but this was indeed a very dire sign. *Could the King possibly be even more foolish...?*

At that moment, one of the attendants formally announced the King, who then ascended the small steps to his throne and took his seat at the head of the room. Harat wasted no time and took several indignant steps toward the throne.

"Your Majesty, I *again* respectfully request that we put together some groups to ensure that – "

"Silence!" shrieked Ambassador Artaban, his shrill utterance shocking everyone in the throne room. "The days of addressing your King without the reverence he is due are over. From now on, Captain Harat, you will adhere to the strictest of traditions. Do not speak to your King unless you are asked to speak."

Harat's rage was palpable, though he made no reply. No one ever dared speak to the Captain of the Royal Guard with such insolence. It was something he had no interest in getting accustomed to.

"Now then," said King Tigran in a conciliatory tone, "Captain Harat is an old and celebrated war hero of our kingdom. I will not hold him in contempt for speaking out of line. However," he continued, turning to face Harat but without meeting his eyes, "Armenia is no longer at war and, sadly, we no longer need your kind of hero. Now is a time of peace and progress. And so, I thank you, Captain, for your many years of most commendable service to the Crown... but I am now dismissing you from your service...and I am disbanding the Royal Guard; I believe it is time for fresh faces protecting the throne and its interests."

For a few moments, there was nothing but shocked silence throughout. Then slowly, the Royal Guardsmen regained their senses with gulps of surprise and disbelief; a few turned to Harat who stood in stony silence, clearly incensed, but saying nothing. Then, through the guardsmen ranks, surprise turned to mumblings and angry whispers.

Harat knew he should silence them, remind them that title or not, job or not, they were still men of honor. But he could not muster the effort, as his mind was racing through all that this act of the new King would change.

At last, Harat spoke.

"What about the protection of the Prince, your son? There has already been one attempt – "

"My son is fine, and will continue to be fine, once he is back from this last idiotic journey north," said the King through gritted teeth. "These noble families you see represented here will finance the protection of the Crown."

Harat shook his head disdainfully. *Yes, they will protect you, and in so doing they will elevate their houses and secure their own protection from a force much greater than their own.*

This was a scheme far worse than inane King Tigran could have devised on his own, Harat was sure. It was no wonder Artaban arrived when he had, and now Mithridates probably no more than two or three days away.

Ambassador Artaban stepped forward, toward the line of angry guardsmen.

"As a show of gratitude," he began, his voice having resumed its usual affected affable quality, "the Crown will give each of the members of the veteran Royal Guard a talent of silver coins. Regrettably, we cannot extend this offer to the rest, but we nevertheless wish to part on amicable terms."

The sum was equal to two years of wages and the men present were momentarily stunned, but it wasn't long before most began muttering and grumbling again. Their loyalty to their Captain and to their kingdom was strong; the money meant little next to the loss of their life's purpose. Harat watched his men with pride; they knew better than to be fooled by such pretenses and deception.

He turned toward the King and his new protectors and offered an exaggerated bow, then began unfastening his armor, each piece dropping to the floor with a loud, cold clank.

"Respectfully, Your Majesty," said Harat, untying is belt and letting his great sword fall to the ground, "you can donate my talent of coins to the Crown."

"How dare you!" cried Ambassador Artaban, who looked at the King to see how he would reply. However, King Tigran remained seated without saying a word, as if hesitant to provoke the Captain further. The Ambassador opened his mouth to again protest this overt display of insolence, but he was interrupted by the sound of more armor rattling and clanging against the cold stone floor.

Many heads, including Harat's, turned to see a few other members of the Royal Guard following his Captain's lead. Within moments, all of the guardsmen were following suit. Harat's heart swelled with pride even as he realized the Kingdom he spent his life defending was falling apart like the many pieces of armor that now lay at his feet.

When the throne room had once again regained its silence, the Captain shook his head in disappointment, then turned on his heel to take his leave. One by one, each of his guardsmen did the same. Harat stood at the doorway as his men filed out, nodding to each of them in silent gratitude. The Ambassador was watching the display with incredulous alarm.

"Sire!" he hissed in the direction of the throne. "This is the utmost sign of disrespect!"

Again, the new King made no reply.

The last of his guardsmen through the door, Captain Harat was about to walk out of the throne room for the last time, but out of the corner of his eye he saw Merak, clearly frozen with fright, still standing in the middle of the room. But Harat didn't believe anyone else even noticed him.

"Come on, boy!" he yelled, and instantly Merak regained his senses and obediently ran out of the room as quickly as his short stubby legs would carry him.

Outside the building, the afternoon sun was lighting the road back to the barracks of the Royal Guard. Lined up on either side of the road were more armed men bearing the same contemptible banners Harat had seen inside. *A show of intimidation*, Harat mused with dismay. *This day could not get any worse.*

He urged his men to walk boldly and make their way without fear. The guardsmen obeyed, but as they passed, a few of the armed men jeered and taunted them; then when Captain Harat passed by, most of them were silenced. Not even a disloyal band of men dared to disrespect the warrior that had delivered Armenia more times than they could count.

As they walked the length of the road in safety, Merak nudged Harat.

"What shall we do now?" he asked quietly.

Captain Harat held his head high, but his voice was grim. "Merak, regardless of what the new King said, or any title we may or may not hold, we will do what we always do: everything in our power to be of service to our people and the kingdom."

# Chapter Twenty

The air was completely still. Only the occasional snort or whinny from one of the many beasts pierced the silence. Young Prince Tigran was atop his horse, next to Chief Vahan, with a dozen more riders on each of their flanks.

Across from them was a line of armed Highlander men on horseback, but these were from another enemy tribe. From a distance, Tigran imagined, the two lines facing one another might have looked almost identical and equally matched; but in this short space, with these men just a stone's throw away, Tigran could see they were gaunt and sickly-looking. The winter had clearly been even harder on them than it had on the Tibareni Tribe. The Prince felt sure their suffering would make his task here today all the simpler.

The two lines of warriors faced each other in the middle of a rare patch of flat land which boasted small tufts of young grass that signaled the dawn of spring. The tension was palpable as they all stood, motionless, waiting for one of the men, all of whom were armed to the teeth, to make a move.

"You're certain you want to do this?" Vahan whispered out of the corner of his mouth.

"It's the only way," Tigran replied in an equally hushed voice. "It will be best for all of you, of that I am sure."

Vahan breathed a heavy sigh thick with uncertainty.

"Well, we have come this far. Let's get on with it."

He raised his arm in a gesture of peace before gently nudging his horse forward. Tigran followed a step behind. Two representatives from the opposite line mirrored them, so that the two pairs moved simultaneously towards the middle of the field.

When the men were close enough to speak without shouting, Vahan began.

"I am pleased you are here," he said, with a distinct lack of enthusiasm. "As you can see, we are here as well, as promised."

The leader of the enemy tribe grunted. He was the largest of his men and maintained a proud air, but he, like the others, appeared malnourished and exhausted.

"You promised more than being here," he replied gruffly. "If I recall correctly, you promised 'a proof of peace' – but all I see here are dozens of your men, armed for battle."

Tigran looked at Vahan, who was doing a poor job of concealing his hostility toward these rogue Highlanders. Before Vahan could make a reply that would certainly ruin the mission, Tigran jumped in.

"And we have brought you all we promised."

Tigran again looked at Vahan, who wore a grimace of protest. But Tigran nodded to him and Vahan raised a grudging arm in the air. He waved forward a single time and, behind them, the Tibareni riders parted to reveal a dozen mules, each burdened heavily with packs bearing food and supplies.

The stillness of the area was broken as the hungry men stirred and whispered with excitement amongst each other about the bounty that was now just a few strides from their reach. Their leader, for his part, did not disguise his suspicion. He shifted from left to right to get a better look at this "proof of peace" Vahan brought.

"What manner of cruel trickery is this?" he bellowed finally, though Tigran thought he could almost see the man salivating at the prospect of a bountiful meal.

"No trickery," Vahan replied with an air of exasperation. "We want to help you."

"All that we ask in return," interjected Tigran, "is that you not make war on the Tibareni clan, the Mardeni clan, or any of their allies."

"Ha!" sneered the tribal leader's companion. "Then whom will we have to fight?" At this remark, the tribal leader was clearly displeased. He shot his companion a menacing look, which quelled him in an instant.

Then the leader said, "And who are you, an obvious foreigner, to be making promises here?"

"He is the Prince of Armenia," Vahan stated authoritatively before Tigran could make any reply, "and he stands to be king one day."

This time it was the leader's turn to sneer.

"And what is that to us?"

Tigran ignored this display of defiance and said, "I cannot say what may happen in the future, but as we have kept our promise today, I make another promise to you now. If I do become king, I will never ask anything of your clans, and I will never encroach upon your land. I will provide aid when needed and do my part to maintain peace, so long as you make peace with your own neighbors."

"Again," replied the leader, who still seemed distrustful of the Prince's intentions but could not keep his eyes off the gifts that lingered just beyond him, "what do the promises of city dwellers, even if they *are* royals, mean to us? We have always had to fend for ourselves here in these mountains; your words are nothing out here. You have no right to demand anything of us."

Vahan raised his arm again and immediately his men moved back into formation, barring the mules from sight. The rebel leader did his utmost to maintain an appearance of dignity, but he could not conceal a small gasp that escaped from his lips.

Tigran studied him closely; the man was proud, but he was also starving.

"We make requests only; we demand nothing," the Prince reminded him. "Use these gifts to help your people. After we are gone, do what you will."

Tigran then nodded to Vahan.

The Chief was obviously losing patience, but he made one last gesture and again his men parted. Then, several of them began leading the heavily burdened beasts towards the opposite tribesmen. Their leader waited until the Tibareni crossed the halfway point before waving to his men to come and take possession of the gift. He looked over his shoulder to watch the exchange, which went peacefully, some men even thanking the bearers.

A few moments later the opposing Chief turned back to Vahan and Tigran.

"We thank you...but you demand nothing, and so you will get nothing. We make no promises to you; that is not our way."

Tigran nodded, even as Vahan turned away with an irritated huff.

"Just remember," the Prince said, "you are always welcome to join the Tibareni alliance. They will ask nothing more of you than to live peacefully with the other tribes and help one another if you so wish."

The other Chief didn't reply, but he did give Tigran a slight nod before turning back towards his own men. The Prince smiled inwardly; their efforts had not been in vain and he felt proud of himself for seeing it through without violence. He stood his ground and watched as the men finished the exchange of the animals and then, one by one, disappeared into the forested mountains behind them. Once they were all gone, the final Tibareni riders, along with the Prince, rejoined the group.

"Well, I certainly hope that was worth it," Vahan said without conviction.

"After you allied with the Mardeni, your clan and theirs fared well throughout the remainder of the winter, did you not?" Tigran countered. "Are these men not also entitled to full bellies and warm beds? As your tribes grow in strength, your children will no longer starve to death and your young men will survive to become strong warrior-hunters. Peaceable alliances benefit your entire region."

"More of our kin surviving the winter means more mouths to feed come springtime. Moreover, when men don't work for their food, they become indolent, and the winter stores do not stock themselves. Then, come next winter, there are more starving children and more young warriors to attack other tribes for what little food they may have left. We do not have many livable lands up here, we are always bound to clash in bad times. I am not much older than you, Prince Tigran, but I am old enough to have seen such evils in my day."

The Prince lowered his gaze.

"I confess I did not think of it this way."

"You mean well and your efforts may indeed work as you had planned," said Vahan in a softer tone, "but when I say that I hope this was all worth it, you may trust that my hesitance comes from experience, not merely contempt."

Tigran nodded solemnly.

"Come now, Prince Tigran," Vahan said then, and Tigran lifted his head to see the return of that infectious smile of his. "I still believe we deserve a good celebration when we get back. And I daresay, I believe we should hurry. I fear for the maidens of my tribe with that big brute friend of yours roaming around my village!"

They both laughed as they rode away.

———•••••———

Bakar was elated; he had managed to catch the young and beautiful Siran in a rare time of rest. She was just retrieving fresh linens that had dried in the warm late morning sun when she discovered Bakar sitting in the outer village. He was watching a wrestling match between Babandur and the Tibareni village brawler, who was still smaller than Babandur by nearly a hand.

"Siran," he greeted her, "please lay down your baskets for a short time and join me. I am enjoying my oaf of a friend here getting trounced by your smaller fighter."

Siran giggled sweetly and sat down next to Bakar. "I am surprised. Your friend is broad and strong; how can he not be a match for our fighter?"

"Look," replied Bakar, who himself could not help but look at Siran's loveliness instead of the entertainment before him, "Babandur is strong, but he is not as agile as your man. He thinks with his burliness instead of his brain. I believe your fighter is teaching my gruff friend a thing or two about beating one's opponent with finesse and not brawn."

Bakar's small occasion of delight was interrupted by Aro who emerged from the trees with several Tibareni riders he had departed with before dawn. He dismounted and hurried to where Bakar and Siran were sitting together.

Aro's face wore a rare grin as he said breathlessly, "Bakar, there is a valley... It's nearby but nearly impossible to get to for the mountains that surround it... but we saw it today from above... and the horses...! Bakar, there was a giant herd of wild Caspians, more than we could count! Tomorrow we will go back and try to find the means to get down there. Will you come? And where is Prince Tigran? I want to tell him the news!"

Bakar was about to reply that Tigran had not yet returned from his mission of gifting the rebel tribe, but just then he spied over Aro's shoulder the Prince and Vahan entering the outer village from the same path Aro had come from. At the same time, Babandur was striding over to meet them, just recovered from his friendly – if thorough – defeat.

"Prince Tigran, you are returned," hollered Babandur as he approached. "I am still livid that I was not awakened to accompany you today. I had to pick a fight with this Tibareni warrior to console myself, but I was too distraught to win as I ought have."

At this playful comment Siran laughed again. Bakar could have wrapped her up in his arms right then and there, but he was wary of startling her and then, of course, there was the matter of her chieftain brother standing close by.

"Console yourself, Babandur," replied Prince Tigran with a smile. "There was no battle, no fighting; scarcely even a cross word was exchanged."

"It's true," added Vahan. "You didn't miss a thing."

Then he turned his gaze to his sister and, though his face erupted in a sly grin, still his overall expression was far gentler than was his customary demeanor.

"Beloved sister, I am happy to see you have been well cared for in my absence."

"And I am happy that your mission was accomplished without incident," Siran replied as she stood, her cheeks flushing.

"So am I," said Bakar, feeling at once uneasy under Vahan's eye and relieved his friends returned unharmed. Ever since the assassination attempt last year and Harat's charging him with watching over the Prince, Bakar could not stop himself from fretting whenever Tigran went off alone with the Highlanders.

"*I* am not glad," Babandur stated with a studied pout. "If our Prince Tigran continues to have such successes in these parts, how will I be able to practice my new fighting skills?"

Just then, there was a tussle by what looked like a little used path, now overladen with vegetation. Then a ragged-looking messenger materialized from the nearby trees, flanked by two Tibareni tribesmen who were nearly carrying him. Even from this distance, Bakar could see the man was famished and half-dead; but as he came closer, he recognized him. It was a brother from the Royal Guard. All the friends knew him well.

"We found him wandering around past the foothills," explained one of the tribesmen. "He says he knows Prince Tigran and comes bearing important news."

The same look of recognition that Bakar wore crossed the Prince's face as well.

"By the gods! What happened to you?" Tigran cried. The messenger opened his mouth to reply, but all that came out was a hoarse groan. Bakar was certain that if the tribesmen let him go, he would instantly collapse to the ground.

"Get this man some water!" shouted Vahan.

Moments later a tribesman was there with a cup of clean water in hand. He tried to offer the cup to the messenger, but the sickly man was too weak to hold it. Tigran took the cup and held it up to his friend's mouth so that he was able to drink.

When this was accomplished, the messenger managed to find his voice. Though he struggled to speak and even to keep his head up, his voice was wrought with the breathlessness of extreme urgency.

"Sire," he croaked, "your uncle, King Artavazd, he has died. Your father has now assumed the throne. Captain Harat sent me to find you as soon as it happened."

Bakar was shocked. King Artavazd, dead? He looked at Tigran, whose eyes were wide. Neither of them could find the words to make a reply.

It was Aro who broke the silence.

"We have horses at the ready. We travel light, make haste and ride through the night, when we get to Tasha, we can procure fresh horses and supplies, then keep riding."

Vahan nodded. "I am sorry for your loss, Prince Tigran. I will have some of my men travel with you to Tasha. In fact, I will go back with you myself if you so wish."

"No," Tigran replied, "you are needed here. We have accomplished much today and you must stay to ensure this fragile peace holds. But I will send word from the Capital as soon as I can."

"Yes, you do that," said Vahan after an unease pause, "because, Prince Tigran, though you have meddled in our balance here, I still hope your efforts bear fruit. Do not forget my people and what you have started here."

Bakar saw the Prince nod at the chieftain and he himself stole a look towards Siran. She gave him a sad, longing gaze, but then picked up her basket and hurried away. In the moment he watched her go everything else was forgotten, for all he could think of was when he would see her beautiful, peaceful face again.

# Chapter Twenty-One

Ambassador Artaban surveyed the King's chamber, empty except for the new King who slouched uninspiringly in a chair by the window. Small wonder that King Tigran commanded little respect – much less support – from his citizens. The Ambassador was relieved that Tigran had at least acquiesced to intervention from the King of Kings – not that he would have had much of a choice.

"Your Highness, King Mithridates should be arriving any day now. The sooner that happens, the sooner all of this unpleasant discord shall be behind us," began Artaban soothingly. When King Tigran only sighed in reply and turned his head toward the window, he continued. "Nevertheless, I am concerned that you allowed Captain Harat to simply walk out of the throne room after such a display of insolence. No good can come of his open hostility. He is bound to cause trouble."

Tigran's mouth twisted into an expression that very much reminded the Ambassador of a pouting child.

"And what would you have me do," he groused, "put a loyal warrior in irons? Or perhaps expedite *his* eternal slumber, as well?"

Artaban ignored the King's tone.

"Well, you could send him and his men on some far-flung, dangerous mission..."

"You underestimate Harat's intelligence," snapped Tigran. "Just leave him and the guardsmen be. Most of them are old, harmless. All they have left are their tongues. And the younger ones will scamper home to their mothers and be glad of it."

"But will Harat leave *you* be?" pressed Artaban.

He simply could not believe that King Tigran could truly be fool enough to believe Harat would simply stay away.

Artaban decided to change the subject,

"We still have much progress to make in terms of gaining the loyalty of all the noble houses in Armenia. The Houses of Artan and Gazar, for example – they insulted you by neglecting to represent themselves at your Crowning ceremonies."

"Bah, they have paid their due tribute to the Crown," replied the King with a dismissive wave. "I require no more from them at the moment. Those Provinces have always been loyal to my brother and his causes, why should I think they would begin supporting me now? And I would be much obliged, Ambassador, if you would stop trying to create turmoil where, in fact, there is none."

Artaban did not take offense. In fact, he welcomed the King's current state. The nobleman that the King chose to be his chief adviser, Lord Martz of Vaspur Province, had yet to make his appearance, and Tigran was spending his first weeks as king sulking away. It was clear that currently, the King had no interest in making critical decisions.

The Ambassador offered a small bow by way of perfunctory apology.

"Of course, Sire. Your patience and benevolence are humbling, indeed. I shall take my leave of you now."

Outside of the King's chamber were many young men all dressed in their finest armor, the replacements for the Royal Guard. Some leaned idly against the walls while others chatted with one another throughout the corridor. Artaban made his way through the crowd and finally to his own private chamber where he found his attendant waiting for him outside the door.

"Ambassador Artaban," said the attendant with a deep bow, "a messenger brought this for you during your audience with King Tigran."

In his hand was a scroll that bore the seal of the King of Kings. Artaban took it and waved his attendant away as he slipped inside his chamber.

"I hope this is the news I have been waiting for," mused the Ambassador, tearing off the royal seal and unrolling the scroll with a sinister smile.

The missive was short. It said simply that General Sanbel of the Parthian Army and a small faction of the Immortal Guard had broken away from the rest of the cavalry in order to make haste to Armenia. This smaller group was making double time and expected to arrive at the Capital of Artashat just a few days hence, to 'clear the way', with the remainder of the Parthian Army not far behind.

"Ah, very good news indeed!" he exclaimed to himself, his dark smile broadening. "And yet, I think I shall advise the General to make a small detour before coming to the Royal Palace. He could pay a visit to a couple of Noble Houses for us. And in so doing, perhaps we can take care of both of our little problems at once."

———•–••–•———

For the first time in as long as he could remember, Captain Harat struggled to maintain his stern, proud demeanor. He had called for a gathering in secret, outside the Capital and far away from any of the main roads. The fact that the sun was now nearing the mountain peaks on the western horizon told him it was far later than the agreed upon meeting time, yet only stubby Merak and three former Royal Guardsmen had shown up.

The men whispered uncomfortably amongst themselves, batting at the small pebbles that lay by their boots – anything to avoid the awkwardness of facing their Captain.

"We will wait a little longer," announced Harat as he reached for Merak's elbow and pulled him aside, away from the other men.

Merak was clearly surprised by the attention, but the Captain didn't blame him. Never one for combat or danger, or even excessive physical exertion, it was rare that Harat took notice of the boy.

"Merak, I need you for a mission of paramount importance," said Harat, quiet enough to be sure that none could hear. In these backwards times he simply couldn't take the risk. "You must go alone, at once, to the village of Tasha."

"Alone? But Tasha is at least two full days ride from here. I would have to travel through the pitch of night," Merak protested, but feebly.

Harat nodded. "If you leave now, you will be there by midday, day after tomorrow, which should give you plenty of time to intercept Prince Tigran and the others. They will have to stop there on their way back. If they have already passed the town, you should see them on your way there; you must leave as soon as possible so as not to miss them. The Prince cannot arrive back at the Capital unaware of the dangers that await."

At the mention of danger, the color drained from Merak's plump cheeks.

"Perhaps it would be better to wait until first light tomorrow?" he stammered.

"Certainly not! You must make haste," growled the Captain. Leaning closer to the boy he added, "Listen to me carefully; I know you can do this. Time and again, your friends have come to your aid during your years of training for the Royal Guard. This time it is you who can go to the aid of your friends."

Merak seemed to think on what he said, and Harat hoped the boy did not falter.

"What," Merak stammered, "what do I tell them if I find them?"

Harat clasped the boy's meaty shoulder with pride, "*when* you find them," he corrected.

"When I find them," Merak repeated, waiting.

*What indeed.* Harat could hardly believe his first thought was for them to stay in the Highlands and not return, at least until the Parthian army was gone. But he knew the boys well, and knew they would not obey the order. Even if they did hold back a day or two, eventually they would want to see for themselves and return to the Capital.

"Captain?" Merak said.

"Tell Prince Tigran," Harat finally said, "tell him that I advise against it, for my advice is for you all to stay up north for a time, but, if he *must* return to the Capital, he must steal himself into the palace without being discovered. He should ride into the Capital alone, without the others. Tell him the old Royal Guardsmen are being hunted down and that the other boys will be in much more danger than the Prince if caught...Tell them the Parthian army is coming to the Capital. Tell them to trust no one. If the Prince feels he must come, then he must get into the palace and to his father, the King, alone and unseen."

"The King? But Captain..."

"There is no time to explain! If Tigran does not take my advice to stay put, then the only other place he will be safe is inside the Royal Palace. Who knows where the Parthian army will go and who they will kill or capture. You must go now; find the Prince and tell him all that is happening here and all that I have said."

He hated to send the boy, but he also feared Merak would be of little use to the rest of them now. He couldn't know if the first guard he sent had even made it to the Highlands.

Captain Harat handed Merak a small satchel of supplies and pointed him back toward his horse before the boy could protest further.

"I know you can do this," Harat said, "you are a most intelligent young man, do not try to hide it any longer, and be brave when you must. It was a pleasure training you."

Merak's eyes were filled with fear, but he mounted his horse and turned northwest with the utmost urgency. As Harat watched him ride off, he could not help but wish there were someone else to send, but although Merak was not a formidable warrior, he was pure of heart and very wise. His trustworthiness was of precious value during such treacherous times, and Harat was sure the boy's intellect would help him find the Prince and deliver his message.

Begrudgingly, Harat conceded to himself that Prince Tigran would be safest now in the hands of such an innocuous boy, and afterward - if he decided to come back - with his villainous father. Once he was with Armenia's poor excuse for a new king, he would neither be easy prey nor condemned as a member of the "rebels" loyal to Harat. For the time being, at least, King Tigran was no enemy of Parthia and its encroaching army. Harat knew that the same could never again be said of himself. He also knew there were others that could be targets.

Moments after Merak disappeared from view, two more figures came into sight. The Captain and the others instantly recognized them as Royal Guardsmen. There was a palpable sense of relief from the entire group. Not a moment went by before several more men appeared, and then more after them. A few others, not guardsmen, showed up as well: they bravely carried with them the banners of their houses, houses that were loyal to the dead King Artavazd, as a show of opposition against their current king.

In all, there were only about thirty men, but it was enough that Harat could feel pride swelling in his chest once more. Though they were few, the growth of the group had engendered a surge of enthusiasm that percolated between the men.

"Let me warn you now," Harat called out to them, "if you join me today, you are very likely doing so as rebels. Should you prefer not to take this risk, you are free to leave."

The Captain looked about his motley group, but none of them stirred from their spots. Each of them was ready to defend – to die – for the kingdom they so loved. Their loyalty moved Harat so greatly that he required a moment to compose himself before speaking further.

"Very well," he continued at last. "We go south, toward the lands of the Provinces of Artan and Gazar which border Parthia. These are noble families that, like you, have professed their hatred of Parthia. I have lately received word that a part of the Parthian Immortal Guard will cross into Armenia very soon, and likely very close to these houses. These families will be in the most danger. We must do all we can to rescue them and, in so doing, may we inspire two more great Houses to join our cause."

There were nods and grunts of assent as each of the men present remounted their horses and turned toward the road that would lead them south. Captain Harat looked over his thirty men, now only equipped with mismatched, second-hand or borrowed armor and weapons, and was aware there was nothing they could do to survive an attack from the full Parthian Army, but as long as they could get to those southern lands first and deliver those families to safety from the smaller military contingent being sent in that direction, their journey would not be in vain.

# Chapter Twenty-Two

The leader of the Parthian Army, General Sanbel, knelt behind a boulder with two of his scouts. Most of the men in this small faction he had taken away from the main army were Greek mercenaries, rough and ruthless. They were just the kind of men needed for a side-mission such as this - though the General had also brought some of his own Immortals to ensure they were obedient.

Peering over the boulder, he had no trouble seeing several dozen of his men on horseback descending down the shallow ridge toward an unassuming-looking fig farm, at the center of which was the small estate belonging to the Lord of the Province of Gazar. Dawn had just broken and it seemed as if the whole world was still fast asleep. Even the birds were not singing on this hushed, windless morning as the horses trod their way silently along the rows of new plantings toward the plain farmhouse. Their hooves soundlessly plodded through the supple soil, uprooting the Gazar farmers' hard work.

The silence of these early hours at last came to an end when the air was run through with the screams and wails that emerged from the estate house. Moments later, several of his men emerged from the home, themselves shrieking violently. Each of them held a member of the household in his clutches, most of whom were women and children. The General looked on as his men beat them, but still they screamed, begging for deliverance and mercy.

His other men were still inside the house, laying waste to the structure and pillaging whatever they could carry that appeared to be of value. Every so often one would emerge, arms heavy laden, and carry his plunder back to a cart a few of their horses were pulling. Thus they walked to and from the house, past its occupants in the process of being tortured to within an inch of their lives, without so much as a glance of concern.

All was going according to plan.

Suddenly, the General became aware of new movements in the woods that surrounded the estate. One by one, men began creeping out of the trees from the north and west. They were a small, ragtag bunch with mismatched armor and a couple of different banners that were of too little import for the General to recognize. In the cacophony, the General's warriors did not notice their stealthy approach.

The scouts whispered to the General in alarm, but he lifted a hand to silence them as he maintained his vigil. The mercenaries were quite taken by surprise at the attack. Too busy tormenting their prey, they took no notice of the twenty men who now surrounded them, swords drawn. His Immortals, however, were quicker to modify their tactics, as he had trained them to do. They tossed their victims aside and drew their weapons.

Just a short distance beyond the safety of the boulder, the small war roared on. To the General's mild surprise, the rebels were, for the most part, adequate fighters. Though they were outnumbered by at least a dozen men, the rebels managed to kill off three of his Greek mercenaries in relatively short order. The scouts looked on in panic, evidently surprised that their General was doing nothing at all to bolster his troops... but the General only smiled calmly.

The trap was sprung.

As the General watched, his confidence faltered only slightly when he noticed one of the rebel fighters take down three of his men – two mercenaries and one of his own Immortals – in nearly one fell swoop. The warrior was old, bearded, and ferocious. This was no doubt the infamous Captain Harat. His fighters were warned not to underestimate his prowess with the broad sword, but evidently their overconfidence had gotten the better of them.

Without hesitating further, General Sanbel turned to one of his scouts.

"Make sure *that* one is kept alive," he ordered, pointing to the old man. "I want him brought to me. The rest of them must be killed."

The scout nodded dutifully and took off running down toward the battle. He managed to catch the attention of one of the Immortals who happened at that moment to be on the periphery as he retrieved his horse for combat. The General watched his scout say a few words to the Immortal who nodded in understanding, mounted his horse, and charged back into the fray. The scout turned away and began creeping back toward his hiding spot, but he was detected by one of the rebels and promptly beheaded.

*Just as well*, thought the General with mild disgust. *Had the simpleton made it back here he would have given away my position.*

Below him, the battle wore on. The Greek mercenaries were in a veritable frenzy, screeching at their opponents and doing their utmost to kill anyone who did not bear the armor of the Parthian Army. The Immortals were much more elegant in their maneuvers, the General observed with a small nod of approval. They were trained to conserve their force so that it may serve them when it was most needed. What sense was there in attacking the children with all of their might when a simple run-through with a sword would do once the more challenging opponents were dealt with?

Though there were several dead on each side, it was becoming clear that the battle was at a stalemate. The men were more evenly matched than the General had anticipated. His Immortals had still not succeeded in sequestering Harat from the rest of his group; he fought valiantly, although the General believed even the old warrior might at last be tiring.

"If only the remainder of the Immortal Guard would arrive," the General said under his breath, "we could put an end to this nonsense. I am getting hungry."

As if his words conjured them right then and there, the rest of the General's army at last appeared over the horizon behind them. Without waiting, they rumbled down the hillside, weapons drawn. As they neared the estate, the influx of men spread itself out around the battle.

The rebels drew inward in a final effort to defend themselves as well as the family from the farmhouse, which now cowered pathetically behind their would-be saviors.

General Sanbel watched the slaughter with impatient satisfaction. This mission was almost complete; it was clear at last that the Armenians definitively had no chance whatsoever. Soon, the General and the Parthian Army could continue on to Artashat. But for now, the insufferable rebels continued to fight, not giving up despite the impossibly bad turn their fortune had taken.

Were it not for Harat, Sanbel would be observing the now-one-sided battle with very little interest. However, Harat's keen swordsmanship and stalwart determination was riveting to watch. Though his men fell all around him, Harat fended off every Immortal that approached him or the insignificant family he would obviously die to protect. As the General watched, the old fighter killed off the last of the Greek mercenaries and then two more of his Immortal Guardsmen, one of whom was on horseback.

But soon enough, Harat was alone, except for two of the family members who clung precariously to life. At last, his Immortals had an easy opportunity to seize him. Not daring to approach the old man, the General's archers drew their bows and arrows and took aim at Harat's legs. One arrow bounced off his shin, the other tore off his small toe.

But instead of howling in pain, like so many of the men – from both sides – had done, the old man roared like a lion, as if the pain of the arrows burrowing into his tissue somehow strengthened him and renewed his will to fight.

*Ah, but apparently even the legendary Captain Harat has his limits* the General thought as he watched Harat's knees buckle at last. He writhed on the ground, still roaring and waving his sword at any who approached him; however, without the use of his legs, Harat was now all but incapacitated.

Several Immortals finally managed to get close enough to place the prisoner in chains, ensuring that Harat's eyes were wide open when the two remaining survivors – a woman begging for mercy and a sobbing teen-aged boy – were sliced, just paces from where he lay, from throat to groin.

The General stood up to take his leave.

He and his one remaining scout regained their horses, which were well concealed in the dense foliage of the forest behind them, and made their way down toward the small estate.

At the bottom of the hill, the General met Harat's white-hot stare. The old captain was chained to a horse that was being led by one of the Immortals. The General could not help but be impressed by his prisoner's force of will; a lesser man would have been dead hours ago.

"I must admit you were correct, Captain," the General said to Harat. "This, our second meeting, was truly more captivating. But I hope to see you again later, as well."

Sanbel turned his horse onto the road to Artashat, followed closely behind by his scout and the Immortal escorting Harat. Behind them, the remaining Immortals moved past the farmhouse toward the main buildings of the House of Gazar and made quick work of setting what was left of the estate on fire.

The General glanced once over his shoulder to see the last of the corpses being thrown into the flames. Soon, there would be nothing left of this dissenting lord's estate but heaps of black ash next to row upon row of uprooted and blood-stained fig saplings dying in the sun.

# Chapter Twenty-Three

Tigran felt weighted down by a foreboding feeling on the evening they reached the town of Tasha. But when they entered the only Inn, they were once again welcomed by now familiar and friendly faces. Word had just now reached the town with the news of his uncle, but these people did not know Tigran was a prince, they knew him only as a lord from the Capital city.

After they finished an evening meal and made a deal to exchange their horses for fresh ones, the group decided they better rest for the night before continuing. But Tigran could not sleep, so he walked alone through the empty town, gazing up at the stars.

For his entire life he had only known his uncle as the King, and even though they all knew this was coming, Tigran already missed him dearly. Now, his own father would become King, and he would be the Crowned Prince. Tigran was quickly realizing now just how much his life was about to change.

Then he thought of Roya, would these changes help or hinder their relationship? And why had she not written him during the winter? He had just sent out his second letter to her before they left for the Highlands, but he had yet to receive one letter from her. He hoped one would be waiting for him when he got back to the Capital.

Tigran quickly reached the edge of the small town. A full moon provided light on this cloudless, early spring night as the Prince stared towards the south. He couldn't stop thinking of how his life would change in just the next day or two. As the new Crowned Prince, would he still be in the Royal Guard with his friends and Harat? Would he be able to get closer to Parthia and the King of Kings, or would his duties now pull him in the other direction? But most of all, he wondered how long it would be until he could see Roya again.

His mind was still racing when he noticed something moving in the distance. First it was just a small blur, but after a short time, Tigran realized it was a rider. At least he thought it was; a single horse was galloping towards him, but above the steed, Tigran could only make out a small round, bobbing, bouncing mass. A moment later the Prince recognized the familiar riding techniques of Merak. The poor boy was holding on for his life, his hair disheveled and his face red and wet with sweat.

Suddenly that foreboding feeling returned again in the pit of Tigran's stomach and the hairs on the back of his neck raised. Whatever this friend was coming to tell them, could not be good news...

——•••••——

Roya cringed as the pain once again tore through her insides. She rested her hands on her swollen belly and resisted the urge to claw into herself as the midwife they were forced to hire busily inspected her below with her thick fingers and warm breath.

Roya was diligently counting down the days and she was sure the baby was due within a few more weeks.

"I am so close now. Is my child in danger?" Roya pleaded, forcing back more questions pressing through her thoughts.

Finally done with her examination the midwife stood over Roya, a sympathetic look in her eyes, and a pleasant smile on her wrinkled face.

"My Lady," the midwife said softly, "I will admit this is not very common. But we will do what we can to alleviate your pain. And please know that there is always a good chance everything will turn out as it should."

Roya sat up and nodded, though she was not appeased.

"A good chance?" Roya repeated as all kinds of scenarios passed through her thoughts.

"Please, my Lady," the midwife replied. "Do not worry yourself unnecessarily, some evil god may hear your fears and make them become real."

Roya thought on that and fought back the pain. "I truly do not know how I could be going through this without you here."

"I appreciate the kind words, my Lady," the older lady replied, not unkindly, "but they are not necessary, it is my occupation. Perhaps we should be thanking your father, for he is paying for my services."

The baby moved again and Roya grimaced as pain shot through her body.

"I will make you a drink to calm you and the baby. It will give you both time to rest," the midwife said, turning towards the hearth.

As the pain subsided again Roya tried to relax as best she could, but the mention of her father did not help. What the midwife did not know was that, though indeed he was paying for her services, since they had no other family or close enough friends here, he was anything but happy about the situation. When Roya first told her father he was furious, condemning her and her 'would-be Prince', and he did not believe her in the slightest when she said he would return to marry her.

But though her father reminded her of his anger every time he could, he also, somewhere deep inside, cared for his only child, his only daughter. And so, her father spent even more time away from the house now, working harder, so that he could afford to pay for the midwife and other added expenses.

Her thoughts then went to the letter she had received a short time ago from Tigran. The Prince indeed confessed his love for her and told her how he could not wait until they met again, but there was no reaction to her own letter. Obviously, the message she received was sent out before he had gotten hers. Roya was sure she would soon be receiving another message from him, or even better, the Prince himself would show up here in the flesh. It was a hope she desperately had to hold on to...

"My Lady, you must be strong when the time comes," the midwife said as she was preparing her concoction, snapping Roya back to the present. "It is only then that any problem will show itself."

The midwife walked toward her stirring something in a cup from which wispy white smoke rose.

Carefully handing Roya the cup, the midwife then said, "Drink this and you will be able to sleep for a time. Be careful, it is still hot."

Roya sipped at the warm broth.

"I thank you again for your service here," Roya said after another sip.

The midwife smiled and bowed slightly in return.

Roya tried hard not to think on the worse that could happen, all she knew was that she wanted her baby to live; there was nothing she was more sure of...

# Chapter Twenty-Four

It was nearly a week now since the fire, and everything that followed went exactly as Artos had planned. Showing his foresight and strength in leadership, Artos declared himself the new ruler of the House of Vaspur and the Province. There was little provocation. His mother had no choice but to stand by her son, as did most all the lords of their Province.

Everyone should now call him Lord Artos.

A couple of lesser nobles that ruled small parts of the Province tried to challenge him, of course, but a visit from Devo and a few of their men in the middle of the night had quickly convinced them to give their new Lord a chance.

News that the Parthian army had entered Armenia was a surprise even to Artos, but the chaos and fear the news brought with it only helped keep the attention off of his quick takeover of the Province.

Today, Devo had gathered together all the men that had ever worked for him and, as Artos stood before his very own small army, his confidence in knowing he had done the right thing soared to new heights. He stepped up onto the make-shift stage Devo had erected for him, and cleared his throat before he began.

"My men, we have reached a pivotal time in our growth together," Artos began. "As you know, ours is one of the wealthiest and most successful provinces in the kingdom. What some of you may not know is that the new king has made promises to my House and to our Province. And for my dead father and brother's sakes, I intend to collect on those promises. Some of you will soon go with me to the Capital, and the rest will help keep our great Province running smoothly."

A stir began among the men as each wondered if he would be one of the fortunate ones chosen to go to the Capital with their leader.

"Do not fret, for as I rise, so shall all of you have a chance to rise!" Artos said. Then in a louder, more confident manner he said, "In my fallen brother's name, I will take control of the barracks and restart the Royal guard, with you, my own loyal men under me!"

There was a cheer then among his soldiers and Artos only continued after it began to subside.

"Then, in my beloved father's name, I will meet with the new King and show him that I am worthy of his ear. I promise you, my loyal followers, that soon your leader will be one of the most important men in the Kingdom!"

The men burst into more cheers, some hugged and others jumped for joy at their new chance for bigger fortunes.

"And as I rise, so shall you all!" Artos shouted over the men to end his speech.

He stepped down from the podium and as he did so, Devo ran up to him.

"The morale among the men is so high right now I believe some would jump off a mountain ledge if you asked it of them," Devos commented.

"They will also not ask to be paid again for a very long time," Artos added.

"Which of them will you bring to the Capital?" Devo asked.

"Pick the most trusted men to stay here in the Province, and the others I would keep close to me," Artos replied.

"I understand, my Lord, I will make it so."

Devo turned to face the men and Artos took his leave. But before he was out of earshot he said over his shoulder, "And Devo, please get everything in place as quickly as you can, I would leave for the Capital soon."

Feeling taller and stronger than ever, Artos walked back to the main house. He would finally be returning to the Capital, only this time he was stronger, he was a lord, and he had purpose.

He thought once again on that day long ago; on the ground, ears ringing and head spinning, he looked up at the face of young Prince Tigran standing over him. *You may have escaped the assassin, but you will not avoid my wrath.*

When he reached the house, his mother was standing out front with his baby sister in her arms. She said nothing. Nor did her face hold any trace of pride or gratitude.

Artos was not surprised, for as he'd grown into a young man his mother and father had surely seen what he was actually capable of, at least in some small ways. Even so, since the fire, his mother had looked upon him with fear and perhaps even a touch of loathing. What she felt or didn't feel; know or didn't know, had no effect on Artos as long as she continued her role as lady of the House – until he was married, of course; then she would no longer be of use to him.

"Mother," Artos said, not unkindly, "was there something you had on your mind?"

She hesitated, then in an emotionless tone asked, "You will leave the province. Is it not still...too soon?"

"What am I to do," Artos replied, "As the new Lord of House Vaspur I have to represent myself to the new king. More importantly, I have to collect on what was promised us, and I must be there quickly to make sure no one else tries to slip in and take all that is rightfully mine...what is rightfully ours... Mother, know that I do this for the good of us all, you and the remainder of our family, for our province."

His mother's expression did not change; was there a hint of anger there, or even pity? Her gaze avoided his eyes as she spoke.

"And you trust the lower lords of the province and these men of yours to...do the right thing while you are gone?" she asked.

And then finally she looked into his eyes, waiting for the reply.

Artos took two slow steps toward her until his face was only a few hands distance from hers. He stared back intently into her eyes.

"I have given my father and brother's former men a wide berth to continue to run the province as they see fit. As long as the regular taxes and tariffs are collected and provided to their ruling House as usual, everyone should be happy. Besides, my own men will always be keeping a close eye on...everyone."

When her expression still did not change and her eyes once again looked away from his. Artos added, "I am confident that *everyone* will be quite loyal while I am away; after all, they wouldn't want the gods to bring down any harm upon them...or the ones they care for most..."

As if to put an exclamation on his point, Artos reached over to rub his baby sister's forehead, then turned and walked away.

# Chapter Twenty-Five

The last person Prince Tigran had expected to see in Tasha was a breathless, crimson-faced Merak. And when Merak relayed the message from Harat, Tigran was dumbfounded, but he remembered the alarm etched into Merak's features.

"Captain Harat is really that concerned for my life?" the Prince had asked.

Merak's frantic reply echoed hauntingly in the Prince's ears, even now, a day a later, as he stood in peasants rags near a stagnant, putrid stream overflowing with trash and feces.

"He is no longer our Captain. Your father and Ambassador Artaban disbanded the Royal Guard only days after your uncle the King breathed his last."

*Why has my father disbanded the Royal Guard?*

Tigran could not stop thinking about it. But even more shocking was the news that the King of Kings and his army was coming to the Armenian Capital. Was this to welcome his father, who was always loyal to the Parthian causes, or was it because the Parthian King believed he could finally, fully, take over Armenia?

He was currently in a part of Artashat that he never seen before, despite it being just outside the palace walls. All around him, servants busied themselves with their duties. Every so often the large gate nearby groaned open and servants passed through with buckets full of waste that they dumped into the foul-smelling stream next to where the Prince was standing.

After procuring an appropriate disguise in Tasha before leaving, he had made it this far without being detected. Tigran had entered the city through a little-used gate, alone, on the pretense of delivering some supplies to a noble family.

Tigran had ordered his friends and the rest of the guards who had come with them to stay behind in Tasha for several days, lest they face more danger than himself if they were caught. Of course, they did not take the command well, and much protest and argument followed, but the Prince's command was the final word in the end. He told them to wait three days, and if they hadn't heard back from him, they could take their chances as they saw fit.

Merak's warning was difficult to believe until Tigran reached the Capital. He'd passed groups of the Parthian army beginning to make camp on the outskirts of the city and now that he saw what had happened to his Capital in such a short period of time, Prince Tigran began to feel more apprehensive than when he'd heard the news of his uncle's passing.

The closer he got to the palace, the more houses he saw abandoned; their windows and doors boarded up. The streets, which just weeks ago were bustling with merchants and children at play, were now all but empty.

Along the stream the Prince noticed several buckets, stained with the stench of rot and feces, lying unattended. Tigran chose two and ventured to the gate, which was yet again swinging open to allow the passing of more servants in and out of the palace. With his peasant's apparel and filthy work buckets, he looked no better than the dozen hapless men and women that surrounded him. He passed through the gate along with several servants, unnoticed, and began making his way to his father.

The further he got into the heart of the palace, the more the sense of foreboding grew. All around him were fierce-looking guardsmen bearing banners he did not recognize. And when he peeked around the corners he crossed, he also saw Parthian soldiers and Lords walking confidently through the palace halls as if they've always belonged there.

He made his way stealthily through the halls he had wandered all his life – though they felt strange and disorienting now – toward the throne room, toward his father. As he did so, he wished desperately to see Harat, though he suspected the last place he was likely to find him now was within these palace walls.

—•——•••——•—

*This day*, mused a sullen King Tigran, *the royal throne room bears witness to something it has never seen before.* He was poised submissively to the left of his own throne; in his place was King Mithridates, the King of Kings, at rest as if every throne in the world was his to occupy. At Mithridates' right hand, a place of greater honor, was none other than their very own, Ambassador Artaban.

Surrounding the three were numerous men from King Tigran's new personal guard, which were carefully comprised of candidates from the four houses most loyal to the new King. There were also several attendants who seemed chiefly intent on doing the bidding of Mithridates and Artaban; none of them paid much attention to King Tigran.

Along the far right wall of the throne room, a handful of representatives from Provinces most favorable to Parthia had shown up and taken their seats; Noble Houses Tigran himself had helped and encouraged for many years now. The rest of the seats sat empty.

King Tigran looked behind them and saw the Royal House Head Servant, the eunuch Theo, standing against the back wall. Tigran couldn't help but snicker to himself; the eunuch was very likely the only person here he could trust.

But outnumbering them all was a division of Parthian Immortal Soldiers which had just lately arrived with their intended conquest: a bruised, battered, and unconscious Harat. Tigran shifted slightly from left to right, craning his neck to catch glimpses of the former Captain between the ebb and flow of the crowd of Immortals. Harat, who was crumpled in a heap on the cold floor, bore numerous wounds on his torso and especially his legs. Some were caked with dried blood and earth; other wounds looked to be hastily wrapped in dirty linen.

A pace or two away, General Sanbel stood watch over his prey. Tigran could not help but smile bitterly to himself. *Even though he is not awake, Captain Harat is an opponent that cannot be underestimated.* In spite of himself, the unhappy King wished vaguely for the old fool to survive whatever outcome awaited them all.

Moments later, Harat stirred with a loud groan and Tigran thought he spied the General flinch, almost imperceptibly. Harat took but an instant to survey his surroundings before struggling, more slowly, to right himself; his perforated leg muscles would evidently not do as they were commanded.

Ambassador Artaban was the first to notice the commotion after King Tigran, who dared not draw attention to the ill-fated former Captain.

"Ah, the traitor has awoken!" he exclaimed to the room in general.

"At last," sighed the King of Kings, as if the tedium of a half-dead hero were simply too much to bear. "Now we can get the matter of this rebel over with and move on to things of greater consequence."

The Ambassador accepted a scroll from one of his attendants, which he unrolled ceremoniously.

"Now then, the charges," he said, looking beyond the scroll to Harat. "This man was a member of the former Royal Guard of Armenia. Upon being retired by the gracious new King of our beloved country, he banded together like-minded rebels to exact revenge upon the kingdom that has fed and sheltered him all his life. On the pretense of heroism, he led his band of rebels to the farm of an innocent Noble family where they attacked and murdered women and children. A unit of the Immortal Guard, which just then happened to be crossing from Parthia into Armenia by way of the same road, tried to save the family and its farm, but it was too late. The innocent civilians perished in the attack, as did all of the treacherous rebels, save this one."

King Tigran held his tongue, but he could feel his face warming with shame. Although there was no doubt that he would sleep better once the fear of Harat's retribution was taken care of, he could not help but wish there was some other way to quell him.

The King of Kings, who was nodding somberly throughout the reading of the charges said with a smirk, "One would think such a courageous leader would be brave enough to die alongside his men."

Artaban smiled indulgently, and Tigran forced out a snort for Mithridates' benefit, one that he hoped Harat could not hear.

Harat looked to be on the verge of protesting, but as soon as he struggled up to one knee, an Immortal was there to knock him back down with the thud of a boot to his ribcage.

"Silence!" shouted the Immortal. "How dare you speak out of turn in the presence of Kings!"

Tigran was hoping the whole matter would be concluded without his involvement, but it was not to be. Once Harat was subdued, King Mithridates turned to Tigran.

"Is it not time for you to affect your first noble action as the King of Armenia?" the King of Kings asked, his tone coaxing and gentle. "You really have no choice but to execute this rebel and post his head on a stake as testimony to how this kingdom tolerates dissents."

Tigran's thoughts raced. He was fully conscious of the power that currently occupied not just his Capital, but his very throne. Harat was never a favorite of his, but even a frightened Tigran had to admit that the old warrior did not deserve such an end. At last, he summoned his courage to speak.

"Great and gracious King of Kings," he said in a voice barely above a whisper, "forgive me, but this man was an honorable soldier of Armenia for many years. I daresay there are few in our kingdom, if any, who would see him any other way. Could we not choose a punishment less...severe?"

Mithridates' conciliatory expression faded into one of disgust, but it lasted only a breath before changing again into a broad, warm smile that somehow frightened Tigran even more.

"The mighty King of Armenia would prefer a more befitting punishment for this hero turned rebel," he mocked with a resonance that reverberated through the entire room.

Tigran could feel Harat's infuriated gaze upon him, and he cast his eyes downward.

"What say you General Sanbel?" King Mithridates then said. "You were the one who captured this killer of innocents, after all."

When General Sanbel spoke, Tigran forced himself to return his attention to the terrible scene before him.

"A fitting end, Your Highness? Put a sword in the traitor's hand, and I shall be most pleased to oblige you with a fitting end."

The King of Kings clapped his hands together like a delighted child, startling Tigran as if there had been an explosion.

"A splendid idea! But remember, if the rebel wins, he must be set free," then the Great King looked directly at Tigran with a juvenile grin, "and King Tigran, I will try not to be *too* disappointed if your man kills one of my best generals. Now someone bring me some wine, we finally have some entertainment!"

Mithridates gave one last cursory look in Tigran's direction, who hesitated for only a moment before he reluctantly nodded an approval, one that everyone in the room knew was not needed.

General Sanbel nodded his head in turn and in an instant, a nearby Immortal Guard relinquished his sword to Harat after helping him to his feet.

Tigran saw Harat wince from the pain of his leg wounds and then ready his sword, which wobbled in his weakened hands. The General offered an indulgent grin and commanded a servant to bring Harat a goblet of water. He followed the demand with a remark that Tigran did not quite hear.

Two or three swigs of water later, Harat seemed miraculously to recover much of his vigor. His stance and his hands steadied and he raised his sword in preparation for battle.

The old warrior, as injured as he had to be both physically and mentally, held his back straight and chest out, with an expression that exuded pride and courage. It renewed a little of King Tigran's enthusiasm and, despite the perilous potential consequences, he found himself rooting for the wrong man...

# Chapter Twenty-Six

General Sanbel was worried that the old warrior was too far gone to make a good battle out of this, and so, he was pleased when he saw the Captain rise up straight and steady his blade in front of him after he took the water. The Captain then challenged him, taking his fighting stance and whispering to his opponent.

"Let's have it then, boy."

Sanbel smiled widely at the taunt; it looked like Harat still had some life left in him. *Good, we shall at least give the King some entertainment.*

The General still did not want to take a chance on the exchange ending quickly, so after they measured each other for a short time he swung wildly from the left, then again from the right. Sanbel realized that his swings would not land, but having Harat dodge the attacks on his injured legs easily caused the dramatic effect desired. All around them, his soldiers roared and cheered as the action began.

The Captain feigned a couple of thrusts with his sword in return. In those moments, the General could feel the laboring breath escaping from Harat's mouth and could almost sense the fire of pain cursing through the older man's legs. Sanbel easily skipped away each time, but only after letting the blade get as close as he dared.

And the men shouted on around them.

Sanbel realized that he still held his smile, so elated was he to finally get the chance to face this old warrior, and end his life. And he swore to himself, it *would* end today.

Harat lunged in with a broad swing to Sanbel's weak side. The

General was again waiting for the last moment before an easy parry, and so he was shocked when the Captain suddenly twisted his body, slicing his sword down as he did so.

The strike instantly opened a bleeding gash on Sanbel's forearm and he grimaced from the pain. The Captain took advantage of his surprise and didn't waste an instant, flipping his blade to his left hand and preforming the exact same maneuver on Sanbel's strong side.

The General transferred his weight and slipped to the side, angling his sword in a blocking position. The tip of his attacker's weapon slid off his own blade with a screech, but still struck home, though this time it was only a graze to his left bicep.

His smile now gone, Sanbel took a long, defensive step backward, and he heard a collective drawing in of breath echo off the throne room walls, realizing that the pair of strikes had stunned their spectators as well. Then the soldiers again began hollering and cheering, even stronger and louder than before.

A safer distance between them now, Sanbel took a moment to gather himself. His body was mostly armored, he was taller and quicker and fresher, yet this old man had just bled him twice with the same tactic. He glanced at the blood dripping off his arms, heard the roars from the men around them, and Sanbel realized that the last thing he had to worry about now was the Captain putting up an adequate fight...

—•—••—•—

When Harat realized the Parthian General was hesitating in order to put on a satisfactory exhibition for his men and King, he had no compulsions about taking advantage of it. Though he was hoping for more than only two small strikes to the arms, Harat was relieved when the General backed off at the end of the assault.

After the short melee he felt the pressure and pain in his knee and bit his lip as he struggled to stay on his feet. Harat didn't have the energy or heart to smile, but the two strikes he just inflicted had taken the smile from his opponent's face. The 'oohs' and 'ahhs' from onlookers circulated low and high around them like rolling waves.

Again, his inner voice cursed him for thinking the Prince would be safe here. Even *he* had underestimated the treacherous lows the elder Tigran could reach. Harat could only hope now that his messages had *not* reached the Prince, or that the Prince did *not* follow his orders, but knowing his men and knowing the Prince, he was sure there was little chance of either.

*Perhaps if I had made peace with those rebel tribes in my lifetime, I would have trusted them enough now to have told the Prince to remain there.*

But there was no time now to ponder his mistakes. The General stood a good two sword lengths away from him now, gathering his senses and peeking at his wounds. The Captain gazed up at his face as he was gathering his own breath in the time he was given. In the many years Harat had spent training warriors, he was accustomed to men trying to hide their fears. He could read right through it. The General was hiding a new-found fear.

Without warning, the General suddenly leapt forward with two reaching stabs. Harat tried to remember to breathe, and not pay attention to his legs begging him to quit while he dodged the barrage of hacks and slashes that followed.

At the end of it they were separated again, and Harat realized he got out of the assault with no additional injuries. But he also realized it did not matter. He could only partially feel his legs now, and wondered how he was even still standing. The pain had reached such heights that it now faded into the background and the Captain began to see shining stars floating in his field of vision.

If his body would cooperate, Harat knew he could take this opportunity to make his own move. He could even imagine the next tactic he would use. But it was of no consequence, for it was all he could do just remain standing.

Harat waited for the next attack, the one that would probably end his life, but time seemed to stretch on forever now. He saw the young men he had trained for so many years ago grow old before his eyes, raise families, and go on to train their own sons. He witnessed again in those moments the infant Prince Tigran in his dying mother's arms, and seeing again his father turn away from the family in his grief. He watched as the years passed and the Prince grew into the young man he was today, and Harat relived all the many proud moments in between.

A smile involuntarily formed on the Captain's lips now. The act opened a dried wound on his mouth and a cracked lip began to bleed anew. The flash of blade approaching him only registered at the last instant. Again, it was only his many years of experience and practice that made him instinctively reel down and away just in time. But the sting on his cheek that followed the parry told him the strike had not totally missed a mark. Harat quickly felt more blood dripping down his face and neck.

The stars continued to float about him and the Captain now felt as if he was floating. *This is it, I am finally done. I am ready.*

Suddenly, through the commotion surrounding him, Harat heard a familiar voice above the others.

"Captain! Father! What is the meaning of this?"

*Prince Tigran!*

Harat's eyes slipped back into focus just as another slash was headed for his neck. The Captain ungracefully fell backwards, but then, with a new resurgence of strength from deep within, he ignored his protesting legs and snapped back onto his feet.

The world spun around him, and he couldn't see the Prince through the blurry crowd that surrounded them, but he felt he was there. Harat realized that all he had left now was to show the Prince one last lesson... never give up, and fight for what you believe in...until the end.

# Chapter Twenty-Seven

Tigran managed to clean some of the filth off of him with a wet cloth in the kitchen on his way to the throne room. There were many servants running about preforming a multitude of different tasks for different people throughout the palace so it was easy for the Prince to blend in, especially since he so intimately knew his way around the place.

Most of the servants, guards and nobles he passed by were either strangers from his own kingdom or foreigners from the Parthian occupiers. Was this how it was to be now? Had he fawned over the Parthian Empire all this time only for the Empire to come and take over his own Kingdom?

*I must not get ahead of myself. I must find out what is truly going on here. It may just be normal for a temporary visit from the King of Kings.* But why then is he here, and without much of an advance warning either, it seemed. It was all rather odd, but he resolved himself not to speculate further until he found out more information.

He reached a little used entry way that led into the throne room from the rear of the chamber. The last guard he passed hadn't even glanced his way, and to his surprise, there was nobody in the hallway now that led to this door.

The Prince slowly pushed on the door. There was a slight creak, but then resistance. The door was being held closed from the other side.

Tigran let out a sigh of disappointment.

*Of course they would at least lock the door that secretly led into the throne room from behind the king. What was I thinking?*

Just as Tigran was about to leave and try to find another way in, the door creaked again, then slid open slightly.

"Is someone there?" a familiar voice asked through the opening.

Tigran's heart jumped. It was Theo, the Chief Royal House Servant! The Prince had known him his entire life, and he knew Theo could be trusted.

"Theo," Tigran whispered, "It is me, Prince Tigran."

"Prince," the eunuch exclaimed in a low voice, "by the gods...are the rest of your friends with you? They could be in grave danger, they are taking out all the old guardsmen they can find."

"No," Tigran replied, "I came alone," and gesturing to the rags he wore he added, "obviously in disguise. What is going on here? I want to get into the throne room."

There was a hesitation, then Theo whispered solemnly, "My Prince, I don't believe this is a good time, you don't want to - "

"Theo," Tigran interrupted as calmly but authoritatively as he could, "as the Prince of this Royal House I command you to let me in." Then he added, "Do not worry Theo, I will be discrete, no one knows I'm here so far."

After another quiet pause the door finally creaked open far enough for Tigran to slip inside.

Immediately, the Prince heard the commotion from the far side of the room. The main open hall of the huge chamber was occupied by a gang of Parthian Immortal guard and other various soldiers of the army. Their backs to the Prince, the men formed a large circle, and were very excited about whatever was going on in the center.

Closer to him was a line of men to the left and right of the King's throne. He could make out, by the back of his embellished crown, that the King of King's occupied the actual throne, while his father sat to his left and Ambassador Artaban to his right. He couldn't tell for sure, but for the time being, it seemed they were also watching or waiting for whatever was going on within that circle to end.

There were some Immortal and Armenian guardsmen about, but also a few servants scurrying around with errands from their masters or passing out wine for the spectators. Tigran was confident he could slip along the back wall and again blend into the scene without notice.

When he turned back to talk to Theo, he was taken aback when he saw a very tall Immortal Guard standing there behind them.

"What is going on here," the guard demanded.

Before Tigran could answer, Theo broke-in.

"I was just instructing this servant on his next tasks," the eunuch said, "tasks for King Tigran himself...*if* it is any of your concern."

Tigran watched as the Immortal looked Theo up and down slowly, a sneer on his lips.

"Go on then," the guard finally said, "but keep it quiet and keep that door closed."

"Of course, my Lord," Theo quickly replied, leaning his back against the door.

The guard turned away from them and from over his shoulder they heard him say, "and I am not *your* lord."

Theo nodded for Tigran to go on, though his face pleaded otherwise.

The Prince nodded back a silent thank you to the servant who had served his uncle King for a lifetime. At that moment Tigran decided he would stay concealed until he knew what was going on within his capital. And right now he was going to find out what was going on with that circle of men beyond.

Tigran walked with purpose along the back wall and stepped down onto the main floor without notice. When a young servant girl was passing him by with four large cups of wine, he grabbed two of them from her tray.

"Apologies," Tigran said firmly, "but I need these for my master." He didn't wait for an answer; instead, he walked towards the center of the hall in a hurry.

When he neared the backs of the rows of soldiers on the outside of the encirclement his heart began to race, and he had to remind himself to stay calm. He walked up to an opening in the last row of men and glided to and fro closer to the center. He still could not see above the heads of the many men in front of him to know what was going on, but Prince Tigran could imagine, now that he heard a clashing of swords coinciding with the up and down cheers of the spectators, that there was a duel between two people happening within.

Tigran was just slipping through another break in the men when he bumped into the arm of a soldier. With an angry, wilding look about his face the bulky warrior raised a fist at him.

Tigran quickly raised one of his arms, putting the full cup of wine he held in the way, but also into full view.

The frown on the guard reversed, and his smile produced rows of crooked, rotting teeth. The fist still hanging above Tigran opened and grabbed at the cup, which Tigran happily released with a slight bow.

As the man turned to down his wine, Tigran quickly pressed on further into the crowd.

The Prince was nearly close enough to finally see when another man gave him a questioning look. Tigran quickly offered him the last cup, which again offered him a chance to slip in closer.

Tigran reached the second row of backs and carefully stepped a bit sideways until he reached two shorter men standing beside each other. He could see the back of a tall, armored man, his long black hair tied in a bun behind his head. Ahead of this man should be the opponent, who Tigran could not see.

*Two Parthian Guardsmen fighting each other in the throne room?*

It wasn't the craziest thing that could be happening, but why would the Kings tolerate such a thing in the throne room? Surely the Great Parthian Empire was above *that* sort of entertainment? *These must be important men.*

Tigran watched as the back of the man he *could* see suddenly lunged away from him, then came another clash of swords followed by the screech of metal on metal as the blades slid along each other.

When the aggressor's back turned after the exchange Tigran saw his opponent. Blood caked the side of the man's head and he stood wobbling on crooked legs coated in dried blood. Tigran could make out a balding head at the center of a coating of blood-stained white hair.

*Who?*

Tigran moved in closer, no longer noticing the soldiers around him.
*What?*

Tigran stared intently at the old man in the center who was barely able to stand, injured beyond belief, even as in his peripheral vision he could see the adversary side-stepping around him, readying himself for another assault.

*That is Harat! That is Captain Harat!*

The Captain just stood there, swaying slightly from side to side, his eyes looking far off into the distance. Tigran realized what was going to happen next, so the Prince abruptly moved himself forward, extending both arms to push away the two shorter men in front of him.

"Captain!" Tigran exclaimed, trying to snap his life-long mentor back to life. Then he turned his head to the dais, "Father! What is the meaning of this?"

His father, a good distance away and above them, looked to be just sitting there, unmoved. Everyone around him hushed for a moment and, in that opening, Tigran made a rush to get to his mentor's side. But his effort was abruptly halted when two guardsmen roughly grabbed at both his arms, firmly holding him back.

The Parthian had his sword arching in for a death blow to the captain's neck. In the last instant, Harat fell back out of the way. Tigran was relieved when the Captain quickly leapt back onto his feet, sword at the ready now.

"All is well," Harat said, just loud enough for Tigran to make out.

The Parthian came in again with another swing of his sword, but the Captain again moved out of the way in time.

The Prince stood there, held in place, still shocked over all that was happening. After riding all night and day and sneaking his way into the palace to see this, he felt as if all the energy he had left was now gone.

"My time is done now, but yours is about to begin. Remember to take care of your people!"

Tigran struggled again, with what little strength he had left, to get free. But his effort was in vain, and all he could do was watch as the Captain then launch into an impossible barrage of assaults.

The Parthian was forced back, parrying and dodging all the way. Soldiers had to move back out of the way, and many of them seemed dumbfounded as to how this duel was not already over. When Harat finished his assault, another wound was added to the ones already filling

the Parthian's arms. Tigran let in a sliver of hope...

...and then, Captain Harat fell to his knees.

The tall Parthian aggressor did not waste another moment, raising his sword and swooping forward for the final blow.

As the tip of the sword began its downward motion Tigran tried to scream out and struggled to release himself again, but he could not hear if any sound was coming out of his mouth, and he could no longer feel his limbs...suddenly his vision blurred and then all went black...

Over the raucousness in his throne room a new panicked voice rose above the rest, a familiar one, reaching King Tigran's ears.

"Captain! Father! What is the meaning of this?"

It was his son, Prince Tigran, dressed like a common servant. His words were screamed as if the General's latest blow – resulting in a wide gash across Harat's cheek – had landed on his own son.

The King sat frozen in place, with only his mind moving.

His son was here; cleverly disguised as a pauper, he had evidently made it through the palace and all the way to the throne room undetected and unharmed. It was a miracle, but it was also a catastrophe.

Prince Tigran, despite his father's desires to the contrary, cherished Harat as a paternal figure. Now he was about to witness his death – his murder, really – which the King of Armenia himself should not have been powerless to stop. He always despised his son's irrationally fierce loyalty to Harat, and witnessing his death would do nothing to increase Prince Tigran's devotion to his father now, especially when the deed was being transacted in his own throne room.

His son's shriek caused the entire room to turn in his direction. Even Harat and Sanbel paused their combat for one bewildered moment.

The Prince seized the opportunity to lunge toward the center of the throne room where Harat was fighting for his life. But two of the Immortals responded instantly to his movement, each grabbing one of Tigran's arms to hold him at bay. The Prince thrashed and screamed until he was red in the face, demanding at once to be released and to let Harat go.

King Tigran turned his face from his son; the agony was too great to bear. Instead, he focused all of his attention on the combat, willing it – one way or the other – to be finished at last.

Harat attacked the General again with what had to be the last remaining scraps of strength still simmering in his aged and deeply wounded body.

The vehemence of Harat's renewed might forced General Sanbel backward and the crowd behind him scrambled to get out of the way.

Harat landed one last blow, a mere grazing wound to the General's left flank. Overall the fierceness of his attack was not nearly what it could have been if the Captain was at full strength, and the General blocked most of his efforts with ease.

It seemed Harat's last reserve of strength was finally spent, and the old warrior then fell to his knees. King Tigran saw a haunting, sinister smile cross the General's face.

The General charged forward, swinging his sword up and behind Harat, and plunged his weapon vertically down the back of the broad neck of one of Armenia's greatest heroes. The Captain did not make a sound as his head and arms fell limp. He was momentarily held in place from the sword in the spine, but after a moment the General unceremoniously pulled out the blade and the body crumbled to the ground.

King Tigran averted his eyes from the horror of the scene before him and stared intently at the floor instead. But it wasn't long until a rapidly expanding pool of deep crimson blood seeped into the periphery of his vision. The elder Tigran squeezed his eyes shut, but he could not block out the wild screams of torment emanating from his son.

Prince Tigran's cries stopped abruptly, and a very composed King of Kings said anticlimactically, "Ah, is that Prince Tigran I see? Has he finally arrived?"

King Tigran forced his eyes open in order to see what had caused the commotion to stop so suddenly. Young Tigran was in the arms of the same two Immortal Soldiers who were already detaining him, only now his son's head was slumped forward and his legs hung limp beneath him. Prince Tigran had apparently lost consciousness from the turmoil and shock of the moment. His father did not blame him in the slightest; he himself felt dizzy and sick to his stomach.

"Did your son know this rebel?" the King of Kings asked innocently. Though the elder Tigran would wager Mithridates very well knew the answer to his own question.

He cast a sidelong glance at King Mithridates who didn't wait for an answer to that question either. Instead, he gazed with the utmost calm over the scene before him – Harat dead in an impossibly large pool of blood, and Prince Tigran unconscious. His victorious General was trying to keep his composure by recanting instances of the fight as lessons for his soldiers, even as his men tended to his bleeding arms.

In that instant it occurred to Tigran that perhaps welcoming the King of Kings into the kingdom with open arms had not been the most prudent course of action. But there was little to be done now. As long as Mithridates chose to be in Artashat, he would do as he pleased. *Perhaps it is still for the best.* But as he wrung his hands and looked one last time at the disgraceful nightmare going on in his own throne room, he knew the last shred of his conviction was gone forever.

# Chapter Twenty-Eight

Ambassador Artaban was relieved when King Mithridates called off the rest of the day's activities in the throne room. After that gory battle, Artaban's stomach had turned. It was no secret that he and the Captain did not get along, but bloody killings were not the Ambassador's style, he much rather preferred to slowly sap the life out of his adversaries.

The King of Kings had pulled the Ambassador and King Tigran to a meeting alone in a private chamber while servants tried in vain to clean up the mess in the throne room.

Two servants brought in trays of food and wine for them, then scurried off. Only King Mithridates indulged himself.

"I am very displeased," King Mithridates began, shaking his head as he chewed on some red grapes. "Most of the seats in your Council of Elders were empty. It is very unfortunate that so many of your noble families dishonor their King, and *me*, in this way."

Artaban shifted his gaze to King Tigran, but the new King only sat there staring at nothing, as if he was sleeping with his eyes open.

"If I may, great King of Kings," Artaban spoke up loudly, hoping to awake King Tigran from his daze, "it is true that our humble people are still divided, but I assure you, King Tigran is committed to bringing the whole kingdom together in the singular effort to better the Kingdom and the Empire."

"Yes," King Tigran mumbled, "a singular effort…"

King Mithridates regarded Tigran with a puzzled expression as he grabbed another handful of grapes and chewed down hard. "I hope so," he finally said, "otherwise, I may have to leave a division of the General's army here to help keep the peace. Armenia will be an important part of the Empire, being the barrier Kingdom that it naturally is now between the Empire and those steadily encroaching, King-less Romans."

The Ambassador was surprised the King of Kings would let slip a rare fear. Nobody really thought of the Romans as any real long-term threat to the Empire, even after they were now effectively taking over Athens and many of the Greek city-states. But if Rome's expansion efforts to the East did continue, they would eventually meet the Empire's interests directly, and Armenia would likely be the eventual buffer Kingdom between them. Perhaps that was why the King of King's had only marked Armenia as a protectorate of the Empire and not an actual vassal, because he wanted that possible buffer Kingdom where they could meet. A buffer kingdom that would strongly have its interests tied to Parthia.

But Artaban dismissed it all from his mind; this was only King Mithridates taking precautions for something that would be years away at best, if it ever happened at all. The King was getting more paranoid in recent years, and this was most likely just part of his new reasoning. The Romans spent most of their time and men fighting each other, or holding those territories closest to their King-less homelands together. Even if they survived, it would be many years until they could be seen as a threat.

"I hope the death of this Captain will not bring about more rebels," King Mithridates continued. "They may now have cause to rally around a common martyr. I have heard that not all of the former Guard have been found?"

Before another awkward silence waiting for King Tigran to respond, Artaban quickly replied.

"We believe it to be less than a dozen men, great King, with a handful of those only young trainees. I doubt they will do anything but flee and hide, especially once news of what happened to their fellow guardsmen reaches them."

"Humph." King Mithridates didn't look too convinced.

"And if I may add, Great King of Kings," Artaban said, "the new guards King Tigran has secured, and the Houses that *are* behind him, are very loyal and strong. It is in their best interests as well to bring about peace and unity and, of course, further the Empire's cause."

"We shall see," King Mithridates replied.

Then he finally showed King Tigran some interest, sneering at him while devouring another fistful of grapes.

"King Tigran, why does your Ambassador seem keener on the happenings in Armenia than you? You have been a fierce and unrelenting champion of my cause all these years. Yet when I come all the way here to welcome you as the new King, I receive merely a few words of exchange from you. This is also very concerning."

Ambassador Artaban thought he was going to have to reach over and nudge King Tigran into responding, but thankfully, he awoke from his stupor.

"Forgive me, Great King," Tigran said sluggishly, "I am still getting over...getting over the death of my brother. But your concerns are understood, and I respect you and the Empire greatly, as I always have. The issues will all be swiftly dealt with, Great King of Kings."

"That is good to hear," King Mithridates said, "especially since the news of those other Houses being attacked. Their refugees will have to be monitored as well."

The Ambassador held in a wince. That information had just been received, and he had hoped to inform King Tigran at a more opportune time.

"What other attacks?" King Tigran asked, just as Artaban assumed he would.

"Unfortunately," Artaban answered in a passive manner, "Four more noble Houses were recently attacked, but the issue has been taken care of."

"Where did this happen? And how is it that these other nobles' Houses were attacked when most of the guard were already captured or killed?" Tigran demanded of him.

He was obviously fully awake now and had decided to take his anger out on him; a good choice since the only other person there was the King of Kings.

"Oh great and wise, King Tigran," Artaban replied, knowing he had to play his part now, "a division of renegade mercenaries hired by the

Parthian army, unfortunately broke off from the main army and decided to raise their fortunes by killing and robbing unsuspecting wealthy families instead. But these traitorous killers have now been captured and eliminated by the Parthian Immortals."

King Tigran ground his teeth, his eyes moved to King Mithridates, then back to the Ambassador, before he asked, "Where?"

Artaban sighed. "The incidences occurred within Artan and Gazar Provinces," he replied.

Tigran looked at him with a contemptible understanding, but said nothing else.

"I personally apologize for these most despicable attacks, King Tigran," Mithridates said, "but these things do happen from time to time when moving such an army. It is a lesson though, you cannot trust hired help as you can those who have cause to respect you."

"Very wise of you to say, Great King," Artaban said, avoiding the gaze of King Tigran.

"Well, let us get onto more pleasant matters then," Mithridates said then. Artaban could only wonder what he had in mind.

After King Tigran and the Ambassador gave him their attention the King of Kings continued.

"I have a proposal for you King Tigran, a chance to help keep my mind at ease. A way for you and the next generation of kings in Armenia to know there will always be a home for you in Parthia."

Artaban and Tigran now both regarded the King of Kings intently and with puzzled expressions as they waited for Mithridates to continue.

"I propose," Mithridates finally said, "that your son, the new Crowned Prince, come live in Parthia for a time. I am aware this is something that should please him. And what better way to show your loyalty and trust than to have your son learn more of the practices and ways of Parthia, so that we can ensure that he, too, will one day become a trusted friend-King of the Empire."

There it was. Artaban had thought on it since the time Mithridates first showed interest in Tigran and hinted at the idea. The Ambassador's own final decision was that, for himself, it would be better to keep the Prince in Armenia. After all, why bring in one who could possibly take the ear of the Great King away from him. But Artaban could tell when the King made up his mind on something, so there was little reason to oppose him now.

His hand unconsciously slipped into his robe pocket, gasping the small message scroll inside; the letter from the young Prince's pregnant harlot. He still hadn't known if he would tell the Prince of it, but Artaban was glad now he decided to bring it with him.

When he realized King Tigran was not responding, Artaban said as enthusiastically as he could, "What an honorable and wise offer from our Great King of Kings. This may even prevent any of those old followers of the Captain, and anyone else who has love for the Prince, from attempting to retaliate against King Tigran, knowing that his only offspring and next in line for the throne, is in Parthian hands."

"You can rest knowing that he will remain safe as our guest," Mithridates added, "and as long as you can keep any insurgents in their places, I could even depart here *without* leaving those soldiers behind."

King Mithridates was making it sound like an offer, but Artaban knew he expected only one answer. In this moment King Tigran had a very important decision to make, a decision that could very possibly end his kingship and kingdom. Artaban held his breath in the long pause that followed. Tigran grimaced, obviously realizing now for himself the only outcome.

"A very wise offer, Great King," Tigran finally said, "I would be honored to have my son in your care."

—•——••——•—

It was late the next morning when Prince Tigran opened his eyes and peered around his room through the confused haze of shock. His sleep had been black and dreamless, as though he was dead... as Captain Harat, his mentor and his hero, was dead. He knew that was not a dream.

*Harat. Dead.* The Prince stared without blinking through eyes that did not really see. With effort, he sat himself up in bed. His muscles, like his thoughts, seemed unwilling to exert themselves; to do so would mean once again feeling the full force of his world coming to an end before his eyes. *Harat. Dead.*

Around him, he was vaguely aware of servants, none of whom he recognized, removing the beggar's rags he got in Tasha before he left, then attempting to bathe him in bed with cloths and warm water. Next came the struggle to dress Prince Tigran's heavy, lifeless limbs in garments more befitting his station. All of this was done without admonishment for the Prince's unhelpfulness – or, if there was, he did not hear or notice.

Throughout this endeavor, young Tigran's thoughts crept slowly, menacingly, back into his consciousness. The nightmare had begun with Merak's warning from Harat. No, it had begun even earlier, in the Highlands, with the news of his uncle's death. He had been anxiously awaiting his return to Artashat because it meant that, soon after, he would be heading south to Parthia, to Ecbatana. To Roya. But it turned out that Parthia had come to him, and his return was more violently unpleasant than ever he could have imagined.

Tigran closed his eyes tight, hoping to blot out the reality he woke to. *How could this be? Surely it really was only a horrific dream. Think of Roya. Go back to sleep, and dream of Roya.*

But when his eyes were shut, instead of Roya's intoxicating curves, he saw General Sanbel's sword plunging into the spine of the only man who had ever really been as a father to him. Instead of Roya's bare flesh trembling in ecstasy, he saw Harat's blood pooling around his convulsing, wounded body, and around the boots of the man who murdered him.

He opened his eyes. He was again in the arms of two Immortal Soldiers. He did not know how long they had been with him or when he was removed from his bedchamber.

The Immortals ushered him down the long corridor that led back to the throne room, their arms gripped his own so tightly he felt like a prisoner instead of a Prince of Armenia. *Why does this seem familiar to me?* Tigran found himself thinking as he looked down at his legs, which practically dragged behind him as though they had forgotten how to walk.

The doors to the throne room opened and Prince Tigran's senses were at once assaulted by a shrill voice announcing his arrival, and by the harsh noonday sun streaming through the room's windows, nearly blinding him.

He was led deeper into the room and as his eyes adjusted, he saw that the floor was still stained a deep, grotesque brown – a terrible reminder of Harat's gruesome and unwarranted end. The Prince willed his neck muscles to lift his head and eyes away from the sight, but then his gaze was set on something no less nauseating: The King of Parthia, again sitting in his uncle's throne, and his own father standing beside him. His own father, the new king, who just sat there and watched as Harat was cut down.

"Ah, welcome back, Prince Tigran," said the King of Kings. He wore a cheerful, friendly smile on his face.

Prince Tigran realized then that he did not know this man at all.

Tigran moved his gaze back to his father. He thought he knew him better, but all he was witnessing so far was a shriveling sheep of a man with a crown on his head. A rush of great anger flowed through him towards his father.

Just then, Mithridates continued. "I believe you will be quite pleased with what your gracious father has proposed. He would have you come to live in Parthia for a time as a show of faith and trust in your ruling Empire. The agreement benefits us all, but mostly you, a young prince who has much to offer – and much to learn from – the mighty Parthian court."

All Prince Tigran's thoughts came to a halt, but he said nothing.

When his mind began to work again the reality of it stuck home. Was he really being exiled to Parthia at a time like this, with Harat gone and his father, who would not meet his gaze, shouldering a responsibility he did not seem ready for? For the first time the Prince began to understand what Harat and his uncle, King Artavazd, had meant all those times they implored him to channel his ambitions and his pride toward Armenia instead of away from it. Tigran had always been intoxicated by the promise of Parthia, always dreamed to be nearer to his beloved Roya... but not like this...

"Poor boy, he is still tired."

It was a nasal, grating voice that spoke next. For the first time, the Prince noticed that Ambassador Artaban was there as well, in addition to a few servants and a dozen Immortal Guardsmen. The Ambassador stood a short distance to King Mithridates' right side, his entire body somehow showing an expression of empathy in the young Prince's direction.

"He will feel much restored once we are back in Ecbatana, which should be soon enough."

King Mithridates nodded.

"In due course, we – along with Prince Tigran, of course – will return to Parthia, where I will welcome the Crowned Prince to my own court as I would a beloved son." He paused for a moment to fix his iron gaze on the Prince. "I know Ecbatana made a lasting impression on you, Prince Tigran, and I understand you already have some close acquaintances there. Your father and I are certain you will be exceedingly happy."

At this, the Prince's father turned to the King of Kings and with some hesitation in his demeanor, said, "I only hope this display of trust will produce many years of peace between us."

He spoke quietly, though it was loud enough for the Prince to hear.

"I am sure of it," The King of Kings replied. Then he clasped his hands and said, "Good then, now, let us move on to other matters."

Prince Tigran was about to speak his misgivings, but the same two Immortals who had brought him to the throne room came alongside him once again. At that moment the Prince realized that perhaps the time to fight for his independence – indeed, for his entire homeland's independence – was passed...or perhaps, had not yet come.

He was a good deal more alert now, but King Mithridates was a powerful and vengeful man who tolerated no measure of disobedience, not even from the loyal and heroic Captain Harat. It was as though all at once, Tigran now truly understood all those little bits of wisdom his uncle and Harat tried to instill into him all his life.

A memory stirred of the shrieking Parthian he had witnessed on his last trip to Ecbatana just before meeting King Mithridates. Now he remembered...

The unfortunate young man had been shackled and was being dragged away in hysterics and sporting fresh wounds on his back. Mithridates had not offered much in the way of explanation, but he had mentioned something about him being a "rotten twig." Prince Tigran looked at the Immortals on either side of him who were now holding onto his arms not unlike how they had held that offending Parthian.

The irony of the situation did not escape Tigran. He was going to be living in Parthia, just as he dreamed. But it was to be as a political hostage, a tool for the King of Kings to keep control. And his own father agreeing to it. Letting the Parthian army occupy the capital, keeping quiet while that Parthian butcher killed Harat...agreeing to his son being taken away...

Prince Tigran knew he was still weak and reeling from the nightmare that transpired not one day ago. If ever he wanted to one day honor the legacy his uncle and Harat had toiled to build and uphold, he would need the fullest extent of his strength and wits about him. He would need to have patience and bid his time, to play along, and one day, someday, the moment would come – but it was not today.

# End of Part 1

# Books in the Series

## Vol. 1: The Rise of Tigran The Great

Part 1: The Road to Parthia

Part 2: Kingdoms and Empires

Made in the USA
Middletown, DE
25 March 2019